# MARRIED
# FOR HIS
# ONE-NIGHT HEIR

# MARRIED
# FOR HIS
# ONE-NIGHT HEIR

JENNIFER HAYWARD

MILLS & BOON

First published in Great Britain 2018
by Mills & Boon, an imprint of HarperCollins*Publishers*
1 London Bridge Street, London, SE1 9GF

Large Print edition 2019

© 2018 Jennifer Drogell

ISBN: 978-0-263-08221-0

**MIX**
Paper from
responsible sources
**FSC™ C007454**

This book is produced from independently certified FSC™ paper to ensure responsible forest management. For more information visit www.harpercollins.co.uk/green.

Printed and bound in Great Britain
by CPI Group (UK) Ltd, Croydon, CR0 4YY

Who knew an unmitigated
hair disaster would turn into
an almost twenty-year friendship?

*Grazie mille* for your amazing input
on this story, Silvano Belmonte.

Our brainstorming sessions
were so much fun!

# CHAPTER ONE

"So, WHAT DID they think?" Giovanna De Luca leaned back against the windowsill of her boss's office, a cup of coffee cradled between her fingers as she absorbed the brilliant sunshine that flooded through the space that served as the epicenter of power for Delilah Rothchild's luxury Caribbean hotel chain.

To look at her, one would have bought the deliberately casual picture hook, line and sinker. That she hadn't just completed the most important assignment of her life, with the decor she'd done for a series of private residences on Delilah's flagship Bahamian resort that would sell for upward of 20 million dollars each. That she was as cool as a cucumber as she waited for the feedback from the initial round of prospective buyers Delilah had met with this morning. But inside, her heart was racing.

Delilah, however, knew better. Knew she was a master at hiding her emotions. "I have verbal expressions of intent for all but two of the villas," she announced, a Cheshire-cat smile curving her lips. "Which will be snapped up in the second round, leaving them desperate for more. Due in large part," she allowed, tipping her head at Gia, "to you. The interiors knocked their socks off, Gia. They were mad about them."

Gia released a breath she hadn't known she was holding on a quiet, even exhale. A warmth flooded through her, spreading from her fingertips to her toes, then sinking deep to wrap itself around the thrumming beat of her heart. She had worked day and night to make sure those villas were perfect. To position them as the irresistible showpiece that would launch the opening of this phase of Delilah's development to critical acclaim. But it went much deeper than that.

The Private Residences at the Rothchild Bahamas had been her opportunity to give back to Delilah everything she'd given to her. To prove the bet the hotelier had made on her had been the right one. To prove to *herself* she could do this—that she could have the career she'd always dreamed of.

She closed her fingers tighter around the coffee cup she held, fighting back the rush of emotion that chased through her. "I'm so happy to hear that," she said huskily. "I know how much this project means to you."

Delilah fixed a laser-sharp, bright blue gaze on her. The woman was legendary for her ability to read a person in under a second flat. Her gaze was warm, however, as it rested on Gia, the bond they'd formed over the past two years undeniable. "You deserve every bit of the kudos. This wasn't personal, Gia, it was business. You earned it with your talent.

"Which is also," Delilah added, rolling to her feet and crossing to the bar, "a cause for celebration." She poured herself a cup of coffee, then turned and leaned against the counter. "I'm having a barbecue tonight to celebrate Junkanoo. Not a big thing—just some friends and a few business acquaintances. A chance to kick back and have a glass of champagne. Put on a pretty dress and come."

Gia shook her head in a refusal that had become customary. "I was looking forward to a night at home. A couple of hours with Leo, a good book and a glass of wine."

Delilah pointed her cup at her. "You need a

life, Gia. It's been two years since Franco was killed. You are twenty-six years old. Working yourself to the bone, then spending all of your time with Leo, isn't any kind of a life."

She thought it was the perfect life. Her three-year-old son, Leo, meant everything to her. She had walked away from her family—one of the most powerful organized-crime syndicates in America—to protect him. He was happy and thriving and that was all that mattered.

"Besides," Delilah added, a crafty smile curving her mouth, "there is someone I want you to meet. A friend of mine who does international financing. He is single for the first time in forever, he is nice and he is loaded. *And*," she added on a low purr, "he is divine-looking. As in drop-dead gorgeous."

As in the last thing she was looking for. Getting involved with another rich, powerful man after her life had been ruled by such men held no interest for her. Getting involved with *any* man wasn't in her plans after her disastrous marriage to Franco. But she would never say that to Delilah, the woman who had given her sanctuary in the months following her husband's targeted assassination. Who had been her lifeline ever since.

"I'm not interested in being set up," she said firmly. "But maybe you are right about me needing to get out. Will I know anyone there?"

Delilah named a couple of women she worked with at the hotel. Gia thought about the hours after Leo went to bed, when there was no escape from the loneliness that had consumed her life. When she missed her mother so much it felt like her insides were being torn out. When what-ifs infiltrated her head, taunting her with what might have been.

Her stomach curled. She didn't want to go there tonight. Her new life was wonderful— *amazing*—and everything she'd always dreamed of. She was moving forward, not backward. Delilah was right, it was time for her to start living again. Tonight would be the perfect opportunity to dip her toe back in.

She lifted an eyebrow. "What should I wear?"

Delilah's eyes flashed in triumph. "Wear something summer fun. Sexy."

Gia shook her head. "I am not letting you set me up, Delilah. This is about me getting out to have some fun. That's all."

"You should still wear something sexy."

* * *

Gia settled for a dress that was neither sexy, nor conservative. A bright coral, with a wrap-front ruffle, it showed off the golden tan she'd acquired while living in the tropics, as well as the smooth length of her legs with its short, flirty skirt.

Anticipation nipped at her skin as she kissed Leo good-night, left him with his babysitter, then walked the short distance from the villa where she lived on Delilah's exclusive Lyford Cay estate, up to the main house. To not have her bodyguard, Dante, tracing her every step was still a novelty she couldn't quite fathom. To step out her front door and not wonder what was going to be on the other side was a peace she couldn't articulate.

But there was also trepidation as she climbed the hill toward the sprawling colonial-style mansion, ablaze with light. She didn't remember what it was like to go out for a carefree evening of fun. Had no idea how to even approach it. Maybe because her life had rarely, if ever, afforded her that luxury.

Tonight, however, she was Giovanna De Luca, not Giovanna Castiglione. She was free.

The barbecue, held on the beachside terrace of Delilah's home to celebrate the popular Bahamian Junkanoo summer festival—a celebration of the arts on the island—was already in full swing when she arrived. A spectacular sunset stained the sky, a fiery pink-and-gold canvas for the festivities as the torchlight climbed high into the night. In the midst of that exotic atmosphere, the guests enjoyed fresh fried fish straight off the grill, rum-based refreshments and a steel band—the classic island experience.

Gia hesitated on the fringe of the group, an age-old apprehension slivering through her. Once upon a time she had been judged for who she was, the family that she came from, rather than the girl she'd been. It had broken her heart—that sense of always being an outsider no matter how hard she had tried. But Delilah quickly spotted her, drew her into the crowd and slid a drink into her hand.

The welcome cocktail, which was heavy on the rum, eased her nerves. As did the handsome financier Delilah introduced her to. He was charming and a gentleman to boot. She might have no intention of getting involved with him, but the clear attraction in his eyes was a boost to her ego, which had taken such a hit with Franco, she wasn't sure the wounds were ever going to heal.

Relaxing into the vibe, the alcohol warming the blood in her veins, she cast an idle glance over the crowd, surveying the new arrivals. A tall, fair-haired male that Sophie, the hotel's glamorous publicity director, was chatting up claimed her attention. Muscular and well-built, he was undeniably commanding in his white shirt and dark pants that showed off every rippling, well-honed inch of him. But it was when her gaze rose to his elegant profile that her breath caught in her throat.

*It could not be. Not here. Not now.*

But it was.

Her heart stuttered an erratic rhythm in her chest, its jagged beat reverberating in her head. Frozen to the spot, her companion's words faded to the background as she absorbed Santo Di Fiore's formidable, charismatic presence. Six foot two inches of lean, hard male, he had the perfectly hewn face and golden hair of an angel. A woman could drown herself in those velvety dark eyes.

And for a night, she had done just that. One

kiss—one perfect passionate kiss on a stormy evening in Manhattan four years ago—had changed everything. An attempt to escape her fate had dissolved into a fire neither of them could extinguish—a hunger that had been almost a decade in the making.

She went hot and cold all at the same time, desperately wishing he was an illusion, because Santo Di Fiore had been her biggest mistake. Her most unforgettable, costly mistake—the repercussions of which had set into motion a chain of events she could never have foreseen. But he had also given her the most precious thing she possessed.

Santo looked up and cast a lazy glance over the crowd. Every muscle in her body seized tight as his gaze came to rest on her, a hint of male interest flickering through his dark eyes, followed by a frown that marred his brow.

Shock descended into fear—a bitter layer of it that coated her mouth. She turned away before he could focus on her, her purse clutched to her chest. *She looked different*. There was a chance he hadn't recognized her, but she doubted that luck would hold. She needed to get out of here *now*.

Spinning on her heel, she headed through the crowd. But before she could make an exit, Delilah descended upon her with one of the investors who'd purchased two of the private residences that morning and her escape route was blocked.

She pasted a smile on her face and tried desperately to pretend that her world wasn't crashing in on her.

He should be on a plane back to New York, stickhandling the most important launch in Supersonic's history, dispensing with the hundreds of emails that had piled up in his inbox while he'd spent the weekend playing in a charitable golf tournament alongside his brother, Lazzero. Instead, Santo Di Fiore was on a tropical island being schmoozed by the current queen of the luxury-hotel market.

Really, he'd had no time. But given he and Lazzero had bet the bank on Elevate—the new running shoe they'd promised investors would set the world on fire—gaining access to Delilah's exclusive clientele list wasn't an opportunity he'd been able to pass up. So after a tour of her impressive flagship property that afternoon, where the hotel maven had expressed her desire to house a half a dozen of his Supersonic boutiques in her hotels, he and Lazzero had been invited to soak up the local atmosphere before flying out in the morning.

He brought his glass to his lips and tipped back a mouthful of Scotch. Under normal circumstances, the delectable redhead, who'd been all over him in far more than a business sense ever since the tour, would have been adequate compensation for the expenditure of time. Instead, he was consumed by ghosts—ghosts he'd thought long ago put to bed. Because surely the sophisticated blonde across the crowd couldn't have been Giovanna. She had beautiful raven-dark hair she'd always worn long and wavy, swearing she'd never cut it short.

He brushed his wayward thoughts aside with an irritated twist of his lips. Giovanna Castiglione had married another man. *They* were over. End of story. That her husband had been taken out in a targeted hit, that she hadn't been present at any of the functions where their social circles might have overlapped since, that she was a widow, *available* now, was inconsequential to him. The Giovanna he'd fallen in love with had been an illusion. She'd never existed.

So why the hell couldn't he get her out of his head?

Lazzero, who'd finished his conversation with a slick-suited real-estate developer, joined him at the bar. "So what do you think of Delilah's offer?" he prompted.

"If we could get the pop-up retail in place in time for Elevate, it could offer us an entrée into a whole different clientele."

"Not a problem." Lazzero dismissed the *if*. "Our retail teams have done it in a month. So we scale—we make it happen. My only question," he allowed, tipping his glass at Santo, "is whose hotel chain do we like more for this? Stefano Castiglione's or Delilah's? They are two entirely different propositions."

A bitter taste filled Santo's mouth. Once he hadn't been good enough for Giovanna—Stefano Castiglione, her father, had made that very clear. Now, Stefano wanted to partner with him because he ran the most buzzed-about athletic-wear brand on the planet, because the famous personalities representing his clothing would make a huge splash at his casinos? Hell would freeze over before he did business with the man who had put those emotional bruises in Gia's eyes.

"Castiglione has a bigger reach," Lazzero pointed out. "Don't let your personal feelings about this cloud your professional judgment."

"What personal feelings?" Santo responded curtly. "The man is a criminal. Just because he's bought half of Washington and Hollywood with his money and influence doesn't mean I want to do business with him."

Lazzero had grown up around the corner from the powerful Castiglione family, just as he had. Knew that along with being one of the most powerful real estate and gambling czars in the United States, his empire reaching from New York to Las Vegas, Stefano Castiglione was reputed to carry darker connections beneath that smooth, charismatic facade of his as the head of an international crime syndicate.

"We aren't doing business with him, Laz." He dismissed the notion with a shake of his head. "End of story."

His brother hiked a lazy shoulder. "I wasn't actually suggesting we do business with him," he drawled. "I was merely yanking your chain to see how you would react. Which was predictable." His brother narrowed his gaze on him. "You're still hung up on her."

"Who?"

"Gia." Lazzero waved a hand at him. "You've gone on a tear through half the women on the planet since her, but you're not even remotely interested in any of them. Take tonight, for instance. You could have had that redhead—the publicity girl. What's her name... Sylvie? Sophie? Instead, you are completely distracted."

"Because I should be back at the office working."

"Says the man who likes to socialize more than he likes to breathe." His brother rolled the Scotch around his tumbler, the amber liquid flickering in the torch light. "So if I were to tell you that Gia is standing behind you it would be of no interest to you?"

He turned to stone. Fingers locking around his glass, he swiveled, his scan of the crowd pinpointing the woman he'd spotted earlier talking with Delilah and another guest. His heart stalled in his chest as he took her in. Confirmed what he'd instinctively known. *It was Gia.*

Clad in a vibrant coral dress that hugged every inch of her curvaceous figure, she was thinner than he remembered, her gorgeous long, dark hair cut into a sophisticated blond bob that gave her a completely different look. Her cheeks were gaunt under her perfect, dramatic bone structure, her eyes deep, dark pools of green that seemed to vibrate emotion.

Exactly as they had that night four years ago when she'd given him her innocence, then walked away, as if what they'd shared had meant nothing. When she'd married another man.

*Turn around*, he told himself. *Pretend she isn't here. Do exactly what you said you would do if you ever saw her.* But he stayed where he was. Gia looked up. She froze as their gazes collided, her eyes widening beneath long, dusky lashes. Like a curtain coming down over her face, the blood fled, rendering her whiter than a sheet.

A midnight storm darkened those beautiful eyes. Twisted something in his insides tight. *Maledizione.* Why tonight? Why here, when she hadn't been seen in public for an eternity?

"Santo," Lazzero said on low note. "She is bad for you. Nothing good ever came of the two of you. Leave it alone."

He was wrong, Santo corrected silently. They had been good that night. *Perfect.* Before she'd torn out his heart. And even though he knew he should stay away, he couldn't seem to do it.

He set down his glass on the bar, ignoring his brother's muttered imprecation as he threaded his way through the crowd toward where Gia stood. But when he got there, she was gone, Delilah and the other guest immersed in conversation. Instinct took him to where Gia stood at the edge of the terrace, looking out at the water, a silent, delicate figure silhouetted against a sparkling, dark blanket of blue.

The image struck him as particularly appropriate, because hadn't it always been Gia against the world? Gia, who'd hovered on the outside, sitting by herself in the high-school cafeteria the first time he'd ever seen her, shunned by her fellow students because of who she was. Because she'd been escorted to and from school by her bodyguards, her friendships vetted and discarded by her powerful father before they'd ever had a chance to take flight.

He would never forget the shy smile that had lit up her face when he'd plunked his tray down beside hers and asked if the seat beside her was taken.

She turned as he approached, as if she'd sensed

his presence, that same invisible thread tethering them together that had always defied reason. Her spine rigid, her face set in a mask he couldn't possibly decipher, she looked haunted. Guarded. *Vulnerable*. It awakened a primitive need to protect inside of him that was as instinctive as it was irrational.

"Santo," she said huskily, unleashing that insanely sexy voice that had haunted his dreams. "I had no idea you would be here tonight."

He came to a halt in front of her. Dug his hands into his pockets. "Delilah is hot on the idea of putting our boutiques in her hotels. Lazzero and I were on the way home from a golf tournament in Albany. She suggested we drop in."

Her long lashes brushed the delicate line of her cheeks. "That's exciting. Delilah has some of the biggest key influencers on the planet on her client list. It would be the perfect partnership."

"We think so." He held her gaze. "I was sorry to hear about your husband."

She inclined her head. "Thank you. It was a shock. It's taken me some time to process it."

He would have bought her cool, collected act if it wasn't for the white-knuckled grip she had on her clutch. The tremor in her voice that dismantled his insides. "Gia," he said softly, stepping forward to sweep a thumb across her jaw. "Are you okay?"

She flinched away from his touch, a quick, reflexive movement that sent a hot rush of emotion through him. "I'm fine. You know I didn't love him, Santo. What my marriage was and what it wasn't."

"I'm not sure what I know and what I don't," he growled, "because you walked away without a word."

"Santo—"

He waved a hand at her. "You dropped off the edge of the earth for two years, only to show up here tonight. Forgive me if I had to ask the question. Old habits die hard."

She anchored her teeth in her lush bottom lip. "I work for Delilah. I have for the past couple of years."

He frowned. "You *live* here?"

She nodded. "You know I never wanted that kind of a life for myself. When Franco died, it was my opportunity to reach out and take everything I had been denied. Delilah," she explained, "is an old friend of the family on my mother's side. She offered to help me create a new life for myself. Gave me a job as a designer for her hotels and a place to stay. No one," she stated evenly, "knows me as Giovanna Castiglione here, they know me as Giovanna De Luca."

*And she wanted to keep it that way.* He struggled to wrap his head around that revelation. "And what does your father think of all of this?"

Her chin hiked, a tiny, but imperceptible movement. "He doesn't know."

He frowned. "What do you mean, he doesn't know?"

"I mean he doesn't know where I am. No one does, Santo. I left the life. I walked away."

*She'd left the life? Walked away?* A surge of astonishment coursed through him. "You *ran* away?"

A fire darkened her emerald eyes. "I am a *Castiglione*, Santo. You know who my father is. What was I going to do? Tell him I wanted out? Tell him I was done? You don't simply walk away from a life like mine. You run and you don't look back."

He ran a bemused palm over his jaw. "So let me get this straight," he began. "You married a man you didn't love because your father decreed it. Because your family means everything to you. And then, when your husband is gunned down in broad daylight outside of his casino, you walk away from that family and all the protection it affords to hide in the Bahamas, where you are open and vulnerable prey?"

"It's been two years. There is no longer that kind of a threat."

There was always a threat. He dealt with it as one of the world's richest men. She faced it because of who she was. But apparently, he conceded dazedly, no one *knew* where she was.

He arched an eyebrow. "And what do you intend to do? Run for the rest of your life?"

"No." Defiance was painted in every centimeter of her ramrod-straight spine. "I intend to live the life I've always dreamed of. I have everything I've ever wanted here, Santo. I'm never going back."

He studied the visible tension etching the sides of her eyes and mouth. Two and two weren't adding up to four here. Something was way off. But he didn't have the opportunity to push it further because Delilah descended upon them with an effusive "Darlings" to talk about the pop-up retail she envisioned for the Elevate launch.

Gia had designed one of the retail spaces he'd

admired earlier on his tour of the hotel, done in partnership with a French high-fashion brand. Delilah thought Gia and his own designers would be the perfect working combination, a suggestion Santo couldn't refute because he'd loved the poolside boutique space Gia had created, an oasis that drew the hotel's clientele in the highest heat of the day. She clearly knew how to meld two distinct brands into a show-stopping, utterly unforgettable space.

Unfortunately, his brain wasn't functioning on all cylinders at the moment as he attempted to follow the conversation, because none of what Gia had told him made sense. Why did she look so terrified if she had the perfect new life? Why would she leave her family to live on her own in the Bahamas when the blood ties that had always bound her had been sacrosanct?

*Why had she not come to him?*

Four years of not knowing, of wondering why she'd left that morning, piled up in his head until he couldn't think of anything else.

He needed closure—once and for all.

But first, he needed answers.

# CHAPTER TWO

GIA PLEADED A headache and escaped the party shortly after her conversation with Santo and Delilah ended. She'd barely managed to keep it together during that encounter with Santo, terrified she'd say something she shouldn't, reveal something she couldn't. But the need to ensure he didn't blow her cover had been paramount.

She'd thought she was safe. That she was finally free after all of this time spent creating a new identity for herself, avoiding any kind of a social life where she might have been recognized. Delilah would have comprehensively vetted the guest list. But Delilah couldn't have known about Santo. No one knew. Apart from her mother and Franco.

She said good-night to Desaray, her babysitter, then went to check on Leo. Her son was fast asleep, his thick, long lashes shading his cheeks, his thumb stuck in his mouth, his sturdy little body curled in the fetal position in his cozy, white-framed bed. She smoothed a hand over his glossy blond hair and pressed a kiss to his soft, scented cheek.

He was so peaceful, her love for him so all-encompassing, he calmed her nerves. But she still couldn't settle enough to sleep, so she changed and got ready for bed, then headed to the kitchen for some warm milk.

She had the feeling Santo hadn't bought her story for a minute. That he'd thought it was as full of holes as she'd known it was. But she was also sure he would never betray her trust—that he would keep her secret. The bigger problem was the business he was conducting with Delilah. If he was considering putting his Supersonic boutiques in her hotels, he would have ongoing interests in the Bahamas. Which would never work.

Dismay clogged her throat. Surely, he would send one of his minions to oversee the project? Chances were, he'd never be here.

But what if he was?

A rap at the door brought her back to reality. Thinking Desaray must have forgotten something, as she was apt to do, she turned off the burner under the milk, padded to the front door and swung it open. "What did you—" She stopped dead in her tracks at the sight of Santo, lounging against the door frame.

Her heart slammed against her ribs. Acutely aware of the expanse of bare skin her silk nightie revealed, she wrapped her arms around herself as the humid, floral-scented air pressed in on her lungs. "Santo," she croaked, "what are you doing here?"

"Getting some answers." He brushed past her into the house before she'd even registered he'd moved. Scared her heart might jump right through her chest, she turned to face him.

"How did you know where I live?"

"Your joke to Delilah about sliding down the hill to get home."

*Dammit.* She bit the inside of her mouth. Really, she hadn't been in her right head. She'd simply been desperate to get out of there.

She had to get rid of him. But how?

She looked up at him, then wished she hadn't, the connection between them crackling like an electrical storm. It reverberated all the way through her, right down to the tips of her toes. Sucking in a deep breath, she corralled her racing thoughts, reaching desperately for the aura of outward calm she had perfected as a Castiglione. "About what?" she enquired evenly, pressing a palm against the frame of the door.

"About why you are really here. What's really going on with you."

"We've been through that already. It is also," she said pointedly, "far too late for this type of a discussion."

"I wholeheartedly agree. I would have preferred to have had it four years ago, but better late than never."

Her stomach dropped. *He wasn't going to give up.* She knew Santo. He was like a dog with a bone when he wanted something. "My head is pounding," she prevaricated. "If you insist on doing this, can we do it in the morning?"

"I'm flying out tomorrow, so no." He gestured toward the living room. "Should we talk in there?"

Panic surged through her veins. "No," she said as calmly as she could manage. "We can do it on the porch. It's cooler out there."

He waved a hand at her. "Lead the way."

She closed the door. Directed him out onto the veranda that ran the length of the villa and overlooked the sparkling midnight waters of the bay. A gentle breeze lifted the leaves of the palm trees, the sweet smell of bougainvillea and frangipani filling the air. But she was too frozen to take in any of it as Santo lounged back against the railing and regarded her with a silent look.

Feeling far too exposed, she wrapped her arms around herself and lifted her chin. "What would you like to know?"

"Why the hell you are hiding in the Bahamas when your mother must be worried sick about you. What were you thinking, Gia?"

She hadn't been thinking. She'd been doing what she'd needed to do to protect Leo. And she'd do it a million times over.

"I left them a note. They know I'm safe."

A flicker of dark emotion moved through his gaze. "Why didn't you come to me?" he growled, the undertone of frustration raking a path across her skin. "You know I would have helped you."

Her lashes lowered. "We were over, Santo. We had both moved on. What was the point?"

"That's a lie," he countered softly. "Why did you leave that morning without saying goodbye, Gia? Why run?"

"Santo," she breathed. "Don't."

His mouth twisted. "Don't ask why you walked

into my arms that night and gave me your innocence? How we could have shared what we shared only for you to walk away and marry another man? Why I woke up the next morning alone, without an explanation? Not a note. *Nothing.*" A lift of his eyebrow. "Which of those things do you imagine confounds me the most?"

She closed her eyes, a hot, searing pain moving through her until it hurt to breathe. "You knew I was promised to him, Santo. You knew I was going to marry him. There was never any doubt about that."

"I thought you'd changed your mind." He threw the words at her in a charged voice that skittered through her insides. "You were emotional that night, Gia. Intensely vulnerable. You didn't want that kind of a life for yourself. You wanted better."

"And then I realized what I was doing. I was getting engaged in front of half of Las Vegas the next night. How was I going to walk away? It would have destroyed my father's honor. His reputation. The Lombardi family's reputation... It was not *undoable*, no matter how much I wanted it to be."

She was Sicilian. A Castiglione. That she

would marry Franco Lombardi, the heir to a Las Vegas gambling dynasty, was a fact that had been cast in stone since the day she'd turned fourteen, when her father had approved the match between his only daughter and the eldest Lombardi son. A match that would cement his empire.

Pursuing the career she'd always wanted, marrying a man she loved and walking away from her destiny had never been options for her, something she'd foolishly forgotten during that impulsive, explosive night with Santo.

There had been no more time left to wonder *what if.* To look for solutions that didn't exist. To want what she could never have.

She drew in a deep breath. Then exhaled as she met Santo's dark, tumultuous gaze. "I convinced myself it would be easier if I simply left," she said huskily. "There was no future for us, Santo. You know that."

He stepped closer, his expensive aftershave infiltrating her senses with devastating effect. "You know what I think?" he murmured, his warm breath skating across her cheek. "I think we will never know because you walked away, Gia. Because it was easier for you to surrender to the inevitable than to face what was between us."

The brush of her bare leg against the muscled length of his thigh unearthed a shiver that reverberated through her. Heat pooled beneath her skin at the memory of what all that hard muscle could do. How it could take her to heaven and back. How it might have been worth every disastrous moment that had followed.

She watched, hypnotized, as his gaze darkened to midnight. As the power of what they created together took hold. One step and she would be in his arms. One tilt of her head and her mouth would be on his.

It would be magical. *Unforgettable*. Which had always been the problem between her and Santo. Because if he knew what she really was, who she was at her core, what she'd *done*, he wouldn't want her anymore.

Her pulse was a frantic, flurried beat she couldn't seem to control, and she took an unsteady step backward. "You're right," she agreed breathlessly, staring up into all that black heat. "It's history under the bridge. You have moved on and so have I. So maybe we should agree on that and call it a night."

A myriad of emotions flickered across his hard-boned face. As if he was debating whether or not to agree with her. She drew in a breath and waited, only to have his attention captured by something behind her, a bemused expression moving across his face.

An ominous thud started somewhere in the region of her heart. Warning bells rang in her head as she turned around slowly to find Leo padding out onto the porch, his thumb stuck in his mouth, his blue blanket trailing behind him. Clearly woken by their raised voices, he directed a big dark-eyed stare at Santo.

Gia stepped toward him, desperate to head off disaster. But there was no way to prevent it. Her son, cheeks flushed from sleep, golden hair ruffled, took his thumb out of his mouth, walked the last couple of steps toward her and held his chubby arms out to her. "Up."

She picked him up and cuddled him close to her chest, her pulse pounding so loud in her ears it was like a freight train running through her head. Santo took in the scene, a frown creasing his brow. The curiosity in his gaze deepened as he stared at Leo. Then his eyes widened, shock flaring in those midnight depths.

It was like looking at two mirror images of each other.

She saw the moment realization dawned in Santo's eyes. Watched the blood drain from his face.

Santo took an unsteady breath as he stared at velvety dark eyes that could have been his own. At the noticeable cowlick that had infuriated all three of the Di Fiore brothers as they'd grown into adulthood. He ruffled the hair of the child in front of him.

*It could not be.* The child could be Lombardi's… Except there was no sign of the angular-faced Italian in the little boy clinging to Gia—there was only the identical image staring back at him. A bone-deep recognition echoed through him—a deep, primal pull in his gut unlike anything he'd ever felt in his life.

And then there was the panic arrowing through Gia's eyes. The stark fear painted across her face as she held the little boy close. The events of the night started piling up in quick succession, bombarding him with the impossible. Why Gia had been so terrified to see him. Why she'd been so anxious to get rid of him.

*Because she'd been guarding a secret she'd spent four years preserving.*

Somehow, he found the presence of mind to pull himself together. "I didn't know you had a little boy." He set his gaze on Gia's stricken face. "How old is he?"

She didn't answer. For so long, so damn long, his heart climbed into his throat. "*Dannazione*, Gia. Answer the question."

"He is three years old."

The earth gave way beneath his feet, any reality he'd thought he'd ever known replaced by a grey haze that threatened to envelop him whole. But the little boy had settled now and was staring at him with big, dark, curious eyes that held the slightest bit of apprehension, and the silence on the porch was deafening.

"Friend?" the little boy whispered, looking up at Santo.

*Friend?* Santo almost choked on the word.

A strangled look crossed Gia's face. "Yes," she murmured. "A friend. And *you* should be in bed." She glanced at Santo. "I need to—"

"Go," he instructed curtly, as if she wasn't about to carry *his son* away from him. As if the world wasn't disintegrating beneath his feet. "We'll talk when you get him settled."

It was the longest ten minutes of his life as he paced the length of the porch, a chorus of cicadas keeping him company as a red haze built in his head. He had used a condom that night—he was sure of it. Except the night had been long, condoms had been known to fail and, quite honestly, the last thing he could remember was Gia stripping down to a skimpy piece of lace and then there had been nothing after that except the hot, sensual explosion that had followed.

Uncertainty dogging his every step, he forced himself to keep a lid on the violent emotion coursing through him until he confirmed what he already knew.

Gia's face was deathly pale when she returned, slipping quietly onto the porch. Dressed now in cropped yoga pants and a T-shirt, she smoothed her palms over her thighs as she came to a halt in front of him.

"He is mine."

The muscles in her throat convulsed. "Yes."

A fury, unlike any he'd ever known, rose up inside of him. He clenched his hands into fists at his sides, attempted to control it, but it escaped his bounds, rising up into his throat until all that emerged was a primal sound of disbelief.

"Santo," Gia said haltingly, "you need to let me explain."

"Explain what?" he exploded. "That I have a three-year-old son you haven't told me about? There isn't one possible reason on this earth you could give me which would explain why you would keep something like this from me."

"Franco," she choked out. "He was going to kill you."

His jaw dropped. "What are you talking about?"

She sank back against a pillar. Pressed a hand against her temple. "I found out I was pregnant a couple of weeks before I married Franco. I was scared, *terrified*. It was a disaster, given the circumstances. I had no idea what to do. I couldn't go to my father—that was inconceivable. So I went to my mother. She told me I had to tell Franco."

"You should have come to *me*," Santo grated out. "It was the obvious choice, Gia."

"And done what?" Fire flared in her eyes. "I was about to marry one of the most powerful men in the country. A pivotal match that would cement my father's business interests in

Las Vegas, which were, at the time, in jeopardy. There was *no way out*."

He gave her a thunderous look. "And so you simply chose to marry Lombardi instead, when you were pregnant with *my child*?"

"There was nothing *simple* about it." She threw the words at him with a ragged heat. "Franco was beside himself with fury. My impulse, my *walk on the wild side* had put the entire partnership in jeopardy." She dragged a hand through her hair. Sucked in a deep breath. "Once Franco had finally calmed down, he told me we would have to make it work. That he would take my son as his own and give him his name. As long as no one ever found out the truth. As long as I never saw you again."

Her eyes glittered a deep green as they lifted to his. "He said if I did, he would find out, he would hunt you down and he would kill you."

*Maledizione*. He couldn't believe what he was hearing. "I can protect myself," he rasped. "You should have come to me, Gia."

She shook her head, eyes bleak. "Nothing would have protected you against him. He had the power to eliminate anyone he liked. He could and would do it. There was no doubt in my mind he would."

His brain buzzed with incomprehension. He understood Gia was intimidated by her powerful, charismatic father. Always had been. It was why she'd married Lombardi in the first place. To humiliate her father by walking away from her marriage would have been unthinkable. But to have passed his son off as Lombardi's? To *lie* to the world about his parentage? It was unfathomable to him.

He fixed his gaze on hers, his fury a hot pulse against his skin. "So you allowed my son to be raised by Franco Lombardi? In the same culture of violence you were brought up in? That same culture of violence you hated so much?"

She shook her head. "I protected Leo. He was never exposed to any of it, Santo. I wouldn't tolerate it. Franco knew that."

*Leo. His son's name was Leo.* He absorbed that mind-boggling fact. "Why leave then? After Franco died? Why walk away from your family?"

An emotion he couldn't read flickered over her face. "Franco was murdered in broad daylight.

I didn't feel safe. I didn't trust Leo's safety with anyone but myself. So I ran."

He bit back the surge of anger that coursed through him at the thought that his son could have been in danger. "To Delilah?"

"Yes." Her lashes lowered. "I had known Delilah from some work I'd done on Franco's hotels. We'd become friends even. I think she always knew there was something wrong with my marriage, but she never said anything. She just said if I ever needed anything, I could come to her. So I did. I explained my situation with Leo, that I didn't want him to live that kind of a life, and she offered to get us out."

"So your mother knows where you are?"

"Yes," she acknowledged. "She's the only one who does. We keep in contact via Delilah."

He rubbed a hand against the stubble on his jaw, brain reeling. Addressed the one point he couldn't wrap his head around. The obvious, simple choice she should have made. "If Franco was out of the picture, what stopped you from coming to me then?"

Color rode high on her delicate cheekbones. "You were with a different woman every week. In a different city on a different continent building Supersonic, Santo. You were not, in any way, prepared to settle down, that was clear. And you had obviously moved on."

"Gia," he growled, feeling himself slipping over the edge of reason. "Tell me the *truth*."

Her beautiful eyes shone a luminous green. "I was afraid," she admitted quietly, "that you would never forgive me for what I'd done. That you might take Leo away from me."

She might have been right. Because right now, all he could feel was the fury burning through his veins. The anger that rose in a wild flood, stripping him of the ability to think.

*He was a father.* He had a three-year-old son. He had missed so many moments, so many milestones, things he would never get back. *Priceless memories.*

It was so far from the vision of the perfect family he'd had for himself, he couldn't even begin to contemplate it. Because that was what he'd always wanted—the family he'd never had. A family like his best friend Pietro's growing up—a warm Italian brood he'd been enveloped in when his own family had been shattered apart. Instead, he had a son he hadn't known about, a woman who'd chosen another man over him, a woman he couldn't trust. A woman with whom the complications ran a mile deep.

He wanted to scream.

Nothing should have prevented Gia from telling him the truth about his son no matter what the circumstances had been. *Nothing.* But he was also smart enough to know that he wasn't in any condition to be attempting rational thought at the moment.

He turned and braced his hands on the railing while he stared out at the sparkling bay. He was supposed to be leaving in the morning. He could safely say that wasn't happening. In fact, he didn't want to let his son out of his sight. But Gia and Leo—who he assumed had been named after her grandfather—were safe for the night, since Delilah's security was second to none. And he needed a chance to breathe.

Gia set a nervous gaze on him as he turned around, clearly attempting to anticipate his next move. "What are you thinking?"

"That I need time to think."

She gave him a beseeching look. "We have a good life here, Santo—Leo and I. He is happy. Well adjusted. He plays on the beach every afternoon and he loves his friends. He won't ever have to suffer the stigma of being a Castiglione."

"He should be a *Di Fiore*." The thick surge of emotion in his voice reverberated through the stillness of the night. "Goddammit, Gia. Have you any idea of what you've taken from me? *Stolen* from me?"

She blanched. Lifted her chin. "Yes, I do," she said quietly. "But I did what I thought was best for Leo."

A harsh sound choked its way out of him. "I know you think you did. That's what astounds me. You think so much like a Castiglione, you don't know the difference between what's right and what's wrong."

A shattered look spread across her face. He ignored it, his brain too full to think. "Here's how this is going to go," he said tersely. "I will contact you tomorrow. At which time you will *be there*, Gia, or I will use every legal resource I have to find you, and when I do, you can kiss your son goodbye, because there isn't a court on this earth that wouldn't award me custody of Leo with your criminal past. The time for running is over."

# CHAPTER THREE

GIA COULDN'T SLEEP. She sat in a chair on the veranda, staring out at the ocean as the deep dark
of a Caribbean night set in with all its requisite
sparkling stars, attempting to absorb the fact
that her secret was out after three long, painful years of keeping it. She wondered what the
ramifications would be, because surely there
would be consequences. Santo's parting speech
had made that clear.

Her stomach curled into a tight ball. She
pressed her palms against it, as if willing it
would smooth out the knots that made it hard
to breathe. Had she really been foolish enough
to think she could keep her secret forever? That
her love for Leo would be enough to sustain the
two of them in this sanctuary she'd created?
That somehow, somewhere along the way, the
truth wouldn't eventually come out?

She'd pushed aside that fear every time it had
surfaced, because Leo's safety had always been

paramount. But her betrayal sat in the back of her mind, festering and dark. Because she'd known what she was doing was wrong. She'd been clear on that, despite Santo's scathing appraisal to the contrary. There had simply been no other way out.

But now, as the guilt pushed its way out into the open, filling her chest with its heavy weight, it threatened to consume her. Her decision had seemed so clear-cut in the moment. Protect her son. Do what was necessary. But after witnessing the naked emotion on Santo's face tonight, allowing herself to acknowledge what she'd stripped him of, it didn't seem so straightforward anymore. It felt selfish. *Unforgivable.*

And couldn't all of this, she acknowledged, hugging her arms tight around herself, have been avoided if only she hadn't had that one weak moment?

She had resigned herself to her marriage to Franco on the eve of her engagement party. Had always known her purpose in life was to cement the Castiglione bloodline through a powerful political marriage, rather than to pursue the dreams she'd had. But running into Santo in the airport lounge they'd both been scheduled to fly out of that night had thrown her into disarray.

A stormy winter night had cast havoc across the eastern seaboard, grounding all of the flights for the evening. Flustered, because she'd known Franco would be furious with her, she'd accepted Santo's offer to find her a hotel room alongside his. They'd ended up having dinner together in the bar of the hotel because the weather had been that bad.

It had been time to catch up properly, both of their lives since high school frantically busy, with Santo building a company and her finishing off a design degree and an internship at a high-end Manhattan firm. They'd kept in touch—a party here, a coffee there—but both of them had accepted the fact that to put some distance between them was the wise thing to do. But she'd never been able to break that bond completely. Santo had been the haven she'd run to when life became too much.

Her thoughts had been a circular storm of emotion that had mirrored the gale-force winds raging outside, the knowledge of what she was about to do, the *fear* of what she'd been about to commit herself to, had clawed at her throat. Her decisiveness had stumbled, replaced by a desperate desire to control her own destiny, if only for one night. For the chance to know what it would be like to be with a man like Santo, who had grown from the eighteen-year-old boy she'd first met into a formidably beautiful man who made her heart race like one of the jet engines that had ceased flying overhead.

They'd polished off an expensive bottle of Amarone over a dinner she hadn't been able to eat, an ever-present, pulsing attraction throbbing across the table between them, a living force she'd never been able to quell. She'd watched Santo extinguish it with that superior self-control of his, her heart sinking as he'd suggested they should both get some sleep.

Which might possibly have worked, had they not ended up alone in a silent elevator as they'd been whisked high into the sky. Had her desperation not reached a fever pitch about halfway there, her fear and frustration closing the distance between them. And then there had only been Santo's arms. A hotel room she wasn't sure belonged to him or to her. A night she would never forget a second of no matter how long she lived, every single piece of clothing they'd re-

JENNIFER HAYWARD                                    51

moved a revelation of what it had felt like to be alive.

One night for herself before she'd married a man she didn't love.

And then had come the harsh reality of morning. Of what she'd done. Of what was ahead—a glittering, star-studded party at the Lombardis' Las Vegas home to announce her engagement to Franco. The day she would officially become his.

Maybe it *had* been easier to run than to face what she'd done. How she'd felt about Santo. Maybe she'd convinced herself he would move on as he always did and she would end up brokenhearted. And maybe, it had been the coward's way out, exactly as he'd suggested.

She finally stumbled to bed in the early hours. She woke bleary-eyed, sure her safe little world was about to be blown to smithereens, and there was nothing she could do about it.

She dropped off Leo at the hotel day care, her heart in her throat as she watched him toddle off to join the others, a smile on his face. *She couldn't lose him.* He was all that she had. It had been them against the world for the past three years. She felt helpless in a way she hadn't in forever and it threw her back to a version of herself she never wanted to be again. Never *would* be again. Powerless. At the mercy of the forces surrounding her.

Delilah, always a lethally accurate barometer of her moods, appeared in her office shortly thereafter. Clad in a brilliant scarlet suit, her perfectly manicured nails colored to match, she looked as impeccable as always.

"Clearly, I have failed in my efforts," she observed, her ever-present coffee cup in hand. "Poor Justin left brokenhearted. Although I think I might have been sabotaged by outside forces. Is there something I should know about you and Santo Di Fiore?"

Gia's stomach curled. "You picked up on that?"

"It was hard not to," Delilah said drily. "The tension between you two was palpable. He was barely paying attention to anything I said."

She swallowed past the giant knot in her throat. "Santo is Leo's father. His *real* father."

Delilah's jaw dropped. Coffee sloshed out of her cup and over the side. She set it down on the cabinet, shaking the liquid from her hand. "I'm sorry. Could you say that again?"

Gia found a napkin in her desk and handed it

to Delilah. "Santo and I had a night together before Franco and I married. We conceived Leo."

Delilah stared at her, gobsmacked. "But how? *Why?* You knew you were going to marry him."

"I was frightened. Scared. Santo was there." She sat back in her chair and drew in a deep breath. "We had known each other since high school. He was a senior in my freshman year. The most popular boy in school—the star athlete everyone loved. *I* was persona non grata. A Castiglione. No one wanted to hang out with me, and even on the rare occasion they did, Dante made quick work of them."

"But Santo," she reminisced, her heart pulsing, "walked right up to my table in the cafeteria. Sat down and started chatting away as if it was the most natural thing in the world that the most popular guy in school would want to talk to me." She sank her teeth into her lip, remembering how tongue-tied she'd been. "I was completely dazzled by him."

"You fell in love with him," Delilah concluded.

"It wasn't so simple. I was promised to Franco. We—" she hesitated, searching for the right words "—became friends. We use to run together in the mornings. Talk afterward in the stands. And there was more," she conceded. "An attraction that grew between us. Dante caught on to what was going on and my father sent a message through him. That I was not a possibility for Santo. That I never would be."

She told Delilah how her friendship with Santo had grown into something special. How he'd been the one she'd always run to. The night her sixteenth birthday party had fallen apart at the seams when her new friend, the one she'd thought might actually become a best friend, hadn't shown up because she'd been forbidden to. The afternoon she'd found out she'd been accepted for a glamorous exchange program to France, only to be told it posed too much of a security risk. The day she'd secured a spot on the track team only to find out her father had ensured it instead with his strong-arm techniques. Santo had always been there.

And then, there had been that night with him that had turned her life upside down. She told Delilah about Franco's fury, and the promise she had made to him to never see Santo again.

Delilah's sapphire gaze deepened with understanding. "Which was why your marriage to Franco was so rocky. Because of Leo."

"Yes."

Delilah frowned. "How did Santo take the news about him?"

"Not well." *The understatement of the year.*

Delilah sighed and took a sip of her coffee. "This is a mess," she said finally. "You know that. Santo is one of the most powerful men on the planet. Does he want his son?"

She nodded. That much was clear.

"Then I would suggest," Delilah advised, "that you attempt to reason with him. It's your only option. And," she added quietly, eyes on Gia's, "you might want to figure out how you feel about him while you're at it. There are clearly some unresolved feelings there between you two."

She intended to ignore the latter piece of advice completely, because Santo clearly hated her for what she'd done. She wasn't sure about the first part, either. The Santo who had walked away from her last night had been a cold, hard stranger she couldn't hope to know. She didn't think reasoning with him was going to work.

But she had to try, because everything banked on her succeeding. Convincing Santo she had done the right thing.

*  *  *

Santo stood leaning against the railing of the terrace of his suite as a stunning pink sunset blazed
its way across the sky. He'd spent the night before attempting to absorb the mind-numbing
news that he had a three-year-old son. Walking
for hours on the beach in an effort to work past
the emotion consuming him. To figure out his
next step. Which had produced a single, yet ir-
refutable solution to the situation he now found
himself in.

He'd gone through it with his lawyer in New
York this morning, his proposed solution the
one his chief legal counsel deemed "the clean-
est one possible." The complex process of having Leo's paternity corrected was another story.
It was a land mine of red tape to negotiate that
left him with a dark cloud in his head. Which
hadn't necessarily been lessened by his brother's parting words that morning.

*You know what I'm thinking.*

*Yes.* And it would never be him. His father had
married his mother, a Broadway dancer, when
she'd become pregnant with his child. Had been
so blindingly in love with her, with the *thought*
of her, he hadn't considered the consequences

of tying himself to a woman who would never be happy. Who had never wanted to be a wife or a mother. Who had married him for his money and then proceeded to make his life miserable from that day forward.

Which was not how his relationship with Gia was going to proceed. His father might have allowed his emotion to rule him, *he* might have allowed emotion to rule him the first time around with Gia, but *this* iteration of their relationship would be based on rationality. On putting their child first.

She showed up at six-thirty sharp, exactly as he'd known she would, because he held all the cards in this unspeakably difficult situation she'd created, and he intended to use them. His plan, however, was momentarily derailed when he opened the door and found her on the threshold.

Clad in a knee-length, olive-green dress with a halter-style top, the soft drape of the material accented her perfect curves, doing particular justice to her amazing backside, which had used to make every boy in school stop and stare. Then walk the other way when they remembered who she was.

Hauling his gaze upward, he refused to allow himself to fall into that trap. He focused, instead, on Gia's pinched face. Bare of makeup, except for a light-coloured gloss on her lips, there were shadows painted beneath her brilliant green eyes. She looked vulnerable. Apprehensive. *Scared.* Which normally would have tugged at his heartstrings, but not this time.

He waved her into a seat. "Would you like a drink?"

She shook her head. Perched herself on the arm of a chair instead. He moved to the bar, poured himself two fingers of Scotch, because he sorely needed it, added some ice, then turned to face her, leaning a hip against the marble.

Gia dug her teeth into her lip, eyes on his. "Santo," she began haltingly, "I don't think we were entirely rational, either of us, last night. It was an emotional discussion. Perhaps we can start over—discuss this situation with a fresh perspective?"

He cradled the glass between his fingers. "Actually," he murmured, with a contemplative look, "I woke up with excellent perspective. You stole my son from me, Gia. You kept his existence a secret for three years, one you would no doubt have continued to keep had it not been for last night. So, from now on, I will be the one calling the shots and you will be the one listening."

She swallowed hard, the delicate muscles of her throat pulling tight. "You need to be reasonable."

"Believe me, this is reasonable after the thoughts that have been going through my head." He inclined his head. "Who is taking care of Leo while you're here?"

"His babysitter. I thought it better we spoke in private."

"And during the day when you work?"

"He goes to the hotel day care."

*"Day care?"* He said the words as if they were dirty, which they were to him, because the idea of his son being cared for by strangers was just that unpalatable to him.

"I work," she pointed out. "I have a successful career, which allows me to support my son. The day care is amazing. Leo loves it. Everyone there is wonderful."

"So he is growing up without a father *and* a mother?"

Her head snapped back, her green eyes firing. "On the contrary. I start and finish work early every day. I spend the better part of the afternoons with Leo, as well as the evenings. He never wants for love or affection, Santo, and the socialization with the other children is good for him. He needs to learn to bond with other kids."

Which she never had. *He*, however, knew the flipside. What it was like to come home to a nanny who had never lasted, and then later, when he'd been a teenager, to come home to nothing at all when his mother had walked out on them.

He'd been thirteen when she'd left after his father's business had gone bankrupt and his family had lost everything—the house, the car, every piece of solid footing he'd ever known. His father busy drowning his sorrows at a local bar, Nico working to support the family, Lazzero off in his basketball-obsessed world, it had been unspeakably lonely to come home to the empty, dingy apartment they'd lived in. So he'd gone to his friend Pietro's instead. Enveloped himself in the freely given warmth that had been bestowed upon him there.

Something Leo was never going to have to do.

"I have no problem with my son socializing with other children," he bit out tersely. "In fact,

I'm all for it, Gia. My issue here is that you have not only deprived Leo of his father, you have deprived him of his extended family as well, because you have walked away from yours and stripped him of mine." He pointed his glass at her. "Nico and Chloe have a two-year-old boy named Jack. A cousin he doesn't even know. How is that *fair*?"

Any color that had been in her cheeks fled. She hugged her arms tight around herself, her eyes glittering with emotion. "I am so sorry," she said huskily. "I am, Santo. I do understand what I did was wrong, despite your opinion to the contrary. But I did what I thought was best for Leo at the time and I would do it a million times over, because I never want him to grow up like I did. As a Castiglione. That was the *only* thing in my head when I left."

He absorbed the defiant tilt of her chin. The fire in her eyes. *That* was what had kept him up all night. The fact that she believed, in her own misguided way, that she'd done the right thing. Because Gia had only ever known one world—a world in which the blood ties that bound her—family, *loyalty*—meant everything. A world in which power and intimidation reigned supreme—except that she'd held no power in that world. In her mind, there had been *no way out*.

He regarded her with a hooded gaze. "What were you going to tell Leo when the time came? The truth? Or were you going to tell him that his father was a high-priced thug?"

She flinched. Lifted a fluttering hand to her throat. "I hadn't thought that far ahead," she admitted. "We've been too busy trying to survive. Making a life for ourselves. Leo's welfare has been my top priority."

Which he believed. It was the only reason he wasn't going to take his child and walk. Do to her exactly what she'd done to him. Because as angry as he was, as unforgivable as what she had done had been, he had to take the situation she'd been in into account. It had taken guts for her to walk away from her life. Courage. She'd put Leo first, something his own mother hadn't done. And she had been young and scared. All things he couldn't ignore.

Gia set her gaze on his, apprehension flaring in her eyes. "I can't change the past, Santo, the decisions I made. But I can make this right. Clearly," she acknowledged, "you are going to want to be a part of Leo's life. I was thinking about solutions last night. I thought you could visit us here… Get Leo used to the idea of having you around, and then, when he is older, more able to understand the situation, we can tell him the truth."

A slow curl of heat unraveled inside of him, firing the blood in his veins to dangerously combustible levels. "And what do you propose we tell him when I visit? That I am that *friend* you referred to the other night? How many *friends* do you have, Gia?"

Her face froze. "I have been building a *life* here. Establishing a career. There has been no time for dating. All I do is work and spend time with Leo, who is a handful as you can imagine, as all three-year-olds tend to be."

The defensively issued words lodged themselves in his throat. "I can't actually imagine," he said softly, "because you've deprived me of the right to know that, Gia. You have deprived me of *everything*."

She blanched. He set down his glass on the bar. "I am his *father*. I have missed three years of his life. You think a *weekend pass* is going to suffice? A few dips in the sea as he learns to swim?" He shook his head. "I want *every day* with him. I want to wake up with him bouncing on the bed. I want to take him to the park and throw a ball around. I want to hear about his day when I tuck him into bed. I want it *all*."

"What else can we do?" she queried helplessly. "You live in New York and I live here. Leo is settled and happy. A limited custody arrangement is the only realistic solution for us."

"It is *not* a viable proposition." His low growl made her jump. "That's not how this is going to work, Gia."

She eyed him warily. "Which part?"

"All of it. I have a proposal for you. It's the only one on the table. Nonnegotiable on all points. Take it or leave it."

The wariness written across her face intensified. "Which is?"

"We do what's in the best interests of our child. You marry me, we create a life together in New York and give Leo the family he deserves."

Gia's stomach dropped, like a book falling off a high shelf. She stared at Santo, horrified, not sure which of his proposals she was most taken aback by. The idea of being forced into another marriage she had no interest in, that it would be with a man who now clearly hated her for what she'd done. Or the thought that he expected her to give up the life she'd made here to return to New York.

She shook her head. "I can't do that. My life is here now, Santo. Everything I *have* is here. Leo loves it. You can't just ask me to give all of that up."

His face was unyielding. "I run a *Fortune 500* company. My business is headquartered in Manhattan. I can't base myself in the Bahamas, however enticing that prospect may be. It is not logical."

She rubbed a palm against the back of her neck. Thought about how completely she'd severed herself from her life. How impossible, how undoable, it would be to simply pick it back up again. Her father had moved the family to Las Vegas a decade ago, when he had concentrated the business on the gambling end of things, but he still had business interests in New York. A collision would be guaranteed.

Her skin went cold. "I can't go back to New York," she said adamantly. "You know what that would mean, Santo. Leo would be exposed to my family. He would become a Castiglione."

A cold fire lit his ebony eyes. "Leo will become a *Di Fiore*. He will be protected as such—as will you. Which leads me to the final part of my offer. Leo will have no contact with your family. *Ever.* Those ties will remain severed. Unless it's your mother on a supervised visit approved by me. If you break that condition, our agreement will become null and void."

*And she would lose Leo.* There was no need to even ask the question. She could tell from the look on his face. Ice formed on Gia's insides. "My father will never tolerate such an arrangement, you know that. My brother, Tommaso, has never had a boy. Leo is his grandson—his future heir."

"Your father has bigger things to worry about." Santo picked up a newspaper that was folded on the breakfast bar and handed it to her. She scanned the page. Found the story he was referring to near the bottom.

Castiglione Thumbs His Nose at Congressional Hearings. Her heart jumped into her mouth. She skimmed the story, which talked about the new attorney general's determination to crack down on the resurgence of organized crime in the United States with a series of congressional hearings set for next month in Washington. Her father, unsurprisingly, had been invited to testify on the subject. He had, also unsurprisingly, refused to attend, electing to take a lengthy sojourn to Calabria instead.

She inhaled a deep breath. This would kill her mother. Her father was everything to her. Her whole life was built around him.

"They will go after his business interests," she said huskily. "My brother, next."

"Perhaps," Santo agreed. "But that would take time. Meanwhile Tommaso will run things in Vegas while your father lawyers up. Which, I'm assuming, he will do."

Undoubtedly. Her father, meticulous with the details in which he protected his empire, would take his time to ensure he was fully shielded against the proceedings before he resurfaced. The battle he'd been fighting against law enforcement had been the bane of his existence, providing an undesirable spotlight when the *famiglia* would prefer to operate in the shadows.

"He will come back," she said flatly. "He will never trust my brother with the leadership. He will make himself impenetrable and then he will plead the Fifth. At which time, he will find out that Leo and I are back. I can't risk that."

"You aren't going to deal with him, Gia. I am."

*Oh, no.* Her heart dropped. That would never work. That would be a disaster. "You know how he feels about you, Santo."

A smile that wasn't really a smile twisted his lips. "That he thinks I'm not good enough for you? Oh, that message came across loud and clear a decade ago. Funnily enough though," he drawled, "we are on an equal playing field now. It will be interesting to see how that plays out."

Her stomach curled at the thought of it. But that fear was quickly replaced by the panic that surged up her throat. "You're going to tell him you are Leo's father."

His black eyes glittered. "You're damn right I am, because that man is never going to set eyes on Leo again. He needs to know that."

Gia felt the world dissolve beneath her feet. This was a nightmare. This could not happen. She needed to do something to stop it before it did.

She covered the distance between them with shaky steps, coming to a halt just centimeters from him. Her heart jammed in her chest at how gorgeous he was in a white shirt rolled up to the elbows and dark jeans that molded to his thighs to perfection. She had always been able to appeal to his softer side. He had never been able to resist her, and right now, she wasn't above using whatever means necessary to prevent him from shattering her world apart.

"Don't do this," she said softly, "You're angry—I understand that. What I did was wrong. But I can't go back there. I'm *never* going back."

His gaze slid to the fingers she had wrapped around his arm, tensile muscle that vibrated beneath her touch. It was, she recorded silently, her second mistake of the past five minutes, because everything went up in smoke then, the slow rise of heat between them palpable as he lifted his gaze to hers, dark as ebony. And, suddenly, she was so tangled up in him she couldn't get out.

"Santo," she murmured. *"No."*

He leaned forward until his mouth was mere centimeters from hers. Her pulse sped into overdrive, threatening to steal her breath. His warm breath fanning her cheek, his blatant masculinity surrounding her from every angle, his heat bleeding into her skin, her knees went weak.

"Nice try," he murmured, "but that isn't going to work this time, Gia. The only possible course of action here is us together, in New York, making this right the way we should have from the beginning. Your damsel-in-distress act no longer wields any power over me."

She took a step back, heat stinging her cheeks. "I was appealing to your sense of reason."

"And so I will give some to you. You are the one who created this impossible situation by not coming to me, Gia. You are the one who passed my son off as another man's child—a complex legal issue that's going to take months to unravel. You are the one who chose to run rather than to face your problems. So *you* need to wrap your head around the fact that *this* is the only option that exists for us."

She lifted her chin. "I'm not *running*. I am *free*, a concept that neither you nor my father would understand."

"Which you will be in New York," he countered. "You'll have every resource you could ever want. The ability to do whatever you please."

"Except live the life I want." She hurled daggers at him with her eyes. "I am not one of your side dishes, Santo, out to plunder your pockets. You know the dreams I had for myself."

He cocked a shoulder. "Stay, then. Take everything you want. But Leo comes with me."

It was a surgical strike. Precise. Deadly. A bolt of fury vibrated through her, her hands clenching into fists at her sides. "And if the courts side with me?" she challenged. "I walked away from my life to protect my son, Santo. I think that's a very powerful testament to the lengths I am willing to go to, to keep him safe."

"Your father is the head of one of the most powerful organized-crime syndicates in the world." Skepticism razed his face. "What kind of a leg do you think you have to stand on? And then," he added deliberately, "there's the part where this would become public if it were to go to court and your life here would be exposed."

She sucked in a breath. *So he was really going to go there?* She hadn't thought he actually would, but *this* Santo, she was realizing, was one she didn't know. Not anymore.

She tried another tact, because apparently, the gloves had come off. "Your father married your mother because she was pregnant with Nico, and look what a disaster that turned out to be. *My* parents' marriage was an arranged match in which my father was never faithful to my mother. *My* marriage to Franco was equally ill-advised. How can you think this is going to work any better for us?"

His jaw hardened. "My parents' marriage was a disaster because my mother was only in it for the money and when that ran out and reality set in, she didn't care enough to stick. *Your* father is an incurable megalomaniac who feeds his ego with power and women. Who never prioritized his family. *Our* marriage will resemble nothing of the sort because we will put Leo first. And," he added, "we have a history to build on together."

"We don't," she rebutted desperately. "We don't even know each other anymore." She jammed a hand on her hip, eyes fixed on his. "Do you really expect me to believe you're simply going to abandon your woman-a-week lifestyle to marry me and we are going to live happily ever after?"

"Yes," he responded, without missing a beat. "Because it's in Leo's best interests that we do. Although you," he said deliberately, "will play an equal role in making this potential marriage successful. It takes two, Gia, another lesson I've learned from the past. So if you agree to my proposal, it will be a real marriage in every sense of the word, because I only intend to do it once."

Her stomach bottomed out. All of this was inconceivable—everything he'd just proposed—but the prospect of becoming Santo's wife in the real sense of the word was the most terrifying thought of all. Because she remembered that night. She remembered how he'd stripped away all of her defenses. How he'd insisted she give him everything. How not one piece of her had remained intact.

Fear rose up inside of her—swift and all-encompassing. And suddenly, it was all too much. Much too much. "I need time to think," she breathed. "You are asking for the impossible, Santo."

"I'm asking for my son. Whom you should have given me in the first place." He downed the rest of the Scotch and set the glass on the bar. "You have twenty-four hours to decide, Gia. Make the right choice."

# CHAPTER FOUR

GIA SPENT THE next morning in a fog. She should have been jumping into a new project—the decor Delilah had asked her to do for her new resort on Paradise Island. It was an exciting, demanding project that would be exceptionally creative, with its fantastical edge. But she found it impossible to concentrate with Santo's ultimatum consuming her thoughts.

She understood he was furious with her. She didn't blame him. But his proposal they marry to give Leo the family he deserved was far from the simple proposition he had positioned it as. Yes, Leo was her priority—had been from day one. But Santo was asking her to walk away from her life for the second time in the space of two years, a life she'd chosen to protect Leo from her past. A life she loved.

Moving back to New York, exposing Leo to the influence of her family, seemed inconceivable. Almost as inconceivable as being locked into another marriage with a powerful man who only wanted to marry her for convenience. For his son. A man she still had unresolved feelings for, the only man she'd ever had those kinds of feelings for, a man who made her feel the dangerous, scary things she'd spent her whole life avoiding because she knew the rejection that came with it.

It seemed like insanity. Because eventually, Santo would resent her for forcing him into a marriage he didn't want and that resentment would eventually splinter them apart, exactly as it had done to her and Franco. Which wasn't an option when she had just managed to put herself back together.

Not to mention the fact that it wouldn't be good for Leo. He would sense the tension between them and it would be damaging to him. She knew it, because she'd lived it every day of her childhood, watching her mother's broken heart.

But what choice did she really have? She could fight Santo in court, tie up a custody battle in international red tape, but that would only prolong the inevitable, because she was quite sure that Santo would win. Which meant her only alternative was to get him to see that marriage wasn't an option for them. That Leo was better off here and that somehow, they could make this work for both of them.

She gave up any attempts at pretending to work by midafternoon, collected Leo from the day care and packed a cooler with some snacks for them for an afternoon on the beach. A half hour later, they were there, a picture-perfect Caribbean scene unfolding around them. The sky a cloudless blue, the sea a vibrant turquoise, the waves a soothing rhythmic roll against the sand—it calmed her fractured senses.

Knees drawn up to her chest, arms wrapped around them, she watched Leo play in the sand from the blanket she sat on as a cool, salty breeze slid across her skin.

"Mommy. *Dig.*" Leo waved a shovel at her, his golden hair falling over his forehead as he crouched in the sand. Her heart contracted at the blindingly bright smile he bestowed on her. How could she give *this* up?

She forced a smile in return, too distracted to contemplate that particular pastime with the chaos going on inside her head. "Give me a minute."

Leo looked past her to the house, his eyes widening slightly. "Friend here."

Her stomach plummeted. She swiveled around on the blanket and saw Santo striding down the beach. Dressed in a white T-shirt and navy blue shorts emblazoned with a red Supersonic logo, every hard-earned muscle from the sports he played nonstop was on display. Aviator sunglasses shielding his eyes, his blond hair spiky and ruffled, he was outrageously good-looking in the jaw-dropping way that had made women lust after him his entire life.

She'd seen them do it time and again at school, some of them discreet, some of them not so much. A phenomenon that had only gotten worse by the time Santo had put Supersonic on the Nasdaq in his midtwenties. Every woman had wanted a piece of the business world's resident golden boy. But even when they'd had success, it had never lasted long with Santo, because although he loved women of all iterations, loved to charm and flirt with them, none of them had ever lived up to his exacting standards of the perfect woman.

*I want a woman who is as interesting inside as she is on the outside*, he'd told her once. *A soul mate*, he'd elaborated on another occasion at a party when yet another candidate had bitten the dust. Which had immediately discounted her. She didn't have the goodness inside of her that Santo was looking for. She was a Castiglione— something that would never change no matter how far she ran.

She was not Miss Arkansas, Santo's last girl-friend, who was a champion of underprivileged kids across the globe. The most stunningly beautiful woman she'd ever seen, *inside and out. She* was a massive work-in-progress.

Her stomach, having picked itself back up again, fluttered against her ribs as Santo dropped down beside her on the blanket. "Friend," said Leo happily, flicking up wet sand with his shovel as he shot Santo another of those curious, big-eyed looks. Gia cringed, but Santo appeared ready for it this time.

"Yes," he said evenly. "Are you having fun?"

Leo nodded and started to dig, keeping one eye on the shovel and one eye on Santo. Gia slid Santo a sideways look, which wasn't necessarily the smartest move because she found herself all caught up in the hard muscle on display. The way his sunglass-clad gaze slid over her in an unapologetically slow perusal from her bare shoulders in the casual sundress she wore, to the tanned length of her legs and her cherry-tipped toes.

"We said five," she blurted out, her bones melting. "My babysitter isn't here yet."

A shrug of a muscular shoulder. "I finished my conference call early. You said you're always on the beach in the afternoon. I thought I'd join you."

Because he'd wanted to see his son. A hot lump formed in her throat as another wave of potent guilt swept through her. She'd compartmentalized her feelings these last couple of years, because it had always been a method of survival for her. Which was exactly what bringing Leo here had been. But now it wasn't so easy.

"Dig," Leo said again, his voice insistent.

Santo took off his sunglasses. Looked at Leo. "Can I?"

Her heart turned over at the thick edge to his voice. Leo gave Santo an appraising look. "Yes," he said finally, and handed Santo a yellow shovel.

Santo took the shovel and joined Leo in the sand. Leo began giving him imperious, one-word instructions, commanding and sure of his domain. They were building, according to Leo, a *supahero's house*. Santo, who had been born with an ingenious brain, as evidenced by the high-tech fabric he'd developed for the sports jerseys that had set Supersonic on the path to stardom, took to the concept like a duck to water.

"He should live in the middle of the mountains," he proposed. "A secret hideaway with a *supapad* to land on."

The idea was met with Leo's wholehearted approval. They began work on the multitiered, elaborate structure. Santo went a bit overboard with the details, heaping sand high around the structure to simulate the surrounding mountains, adding a landing pad for the various aircraft, and a driveway for the high-tech vehicles their superhero would command. Leo ate it up, his eyes sparkling with excitement as he made the requisite sound effects, a chorus of *kapows* and *pishaws* filling the air.

Off went Santo's shirt as the still strong afternoon sun beat down. Leo gave his playmate's powerful, chiseled core an astonished look and asked him if *he* was a superhero. Which made Gia bite down hard on the inside of her cheek, half to prevent laughter and half to prevent other deeper, darker emotions from engulfing her.

Santo was a complete stranger to Leo, but her son was completely entranced by him. Part of it, to be sure, was Santo's charm, because he could beguile any living creature in the universe. But the connection between the two of them was also seemingly innate. It was simply *there*.

A throb built inside of her, curling her insides. Santo was Leo's father. How could she have ever convinced herself that her son would never need *this*? That the love they shared would be enough to replace the bond he and his father could have together?

She'd spent her whole life trying to earn her powerful, important father's love, something she'd never quite seemed to do. Maybe she'd convinced herself that because she'd never had it, Leo didn't need it, either. Maybe it had been a lie she'd been content to tell herself because to stay had been too high a price to pay. And yet, here was Santo ready and willing to offer that love freely to his son. *Passionate* about it.

Her heart expanded until it seemed too big for her chest. She had done such a bad thing.

An unforgivable thing. And she could never take it back.

Leo declared the *supafort* done. Trotting back up to her, he deposited the shovels and buckets in the sand. Gia handed them bottles of water from the cooler. Santo dropped down on the blanket beside her and downed half of his. Leo had a sip, then peered inside the cooler. "Hungry," he pronounced.

"That's my cue." Desaray materialized on the sand behind them, holding her arms wide for Leo, who ran into them. "I'm sorry I'm late. How is my little munchkin?"

Leo giggled and twirled a lock of Desaray's dark hair around his finger. "Good. Bana bread?" he asked hopefully.

"Banana," Desaray corrected. "And yes, Mamma sent some." She slid a curious look at Santo, her dark gaze admiring, before she redirected it to Gia. "School ran late. Sorry. I'll take him inside and get him changed? Give him a snack?"

"That would be perfect." Gia made the introductions to Santo. "I'll go change," she suggested, as Desaray and Leo took off toward the villa, "and we can talk?"

"Why don't we talk here?"

Which probably made sense, Gia conceded. It would be more private. But the romantic setting on the beach combined with the emotion clogging her throat didn't necessarily make for a wise combination. She was about to refuse again when Santo shot her a deliberate look. "Sit down, Gia."

She sat down on the blanket, keeping a safe distance between them as she resumed her pose with her knees curled up to her chest, arms slung around them.

"What's wrong?" Santo asked quietly.

Aside from the fact that he was half-naked and her heart was beating a mile a minute? That he was still the most gorgeous, compelling male she'd ever encountered and no amount of time she'd put between herself and that night seemed to enable her to blank it from her head?

She pushed aside the thought with a determined act of will, because *that* had been what had gotten her into this situation in the first place.

"It was seeing the two of you together," she admitted. "I thought that I was right in the decisions I made. That I could be enough for Leo—

that if I just created a love big enough, *strong* enough, we could be enough for each other. But watching you two just now, I realize how wrong I was in keeping him from you."

An emotion she couldn't read moved through his dark eyes. "You were young and you were frightened."

"Yes," she agreed. "But I still believe Leo is better off here with me, Santo. Away from my family's influence. There are other ways to approach this than marriage. We can find a way to share custody of Leo that works for both of us."

An implacable look moved across his face. "I've already told you, you living here and me living in New York is a nonstarter. I'm not interested in some sort of a modern arrangement, Gia. A *pseudo family*. I want the real thing. I will not compromise on that."

Gia trained her eyes on the sea, her stomach a tight knot. Santo's gaze was hot on her profile. "What?"

"I'm just figuring out who I am. I *like* who I am here, Santo. I am *good* here."

"And you can't be that as my wife?"

No, she couldn't. She would spend all her time trying to live up to the vision of the ideal woman he had in his head, forever knowing she hadn't been his *choice*, she had been his *necessity*. Because whatever they'd once shared, she'd always known that who she was would eventually destroy everything they had. It always did.

She angled her body to face him. "You're ordering me to marry you, Santo. Exactly as my father did with Franco. You are giving me no choice. How can that be the basis for a healthy relationship? How can that be good for *Leo*—two people who are marrying for convenience?"

A dark challenge glittered in his eyes. "Because we are going to *make* this into something good, Gia. We had a friendship once. We can rebuild it."

She absorbed the iron set of his jaw. His utter immovability. Indecision flooded through her. She had been so sure that marrying Santo was a mistake. But after seeing him and Leo together this afternoon, after witnessing what she had denied her son, she wasn't sure of anything anymore.

Santo tipped her chin up with his fingers. "You know it's the right thing to do, Gia," he said softly. "Make the call."

Her stomach twisted. Once again, she was expected to make the *right decision*. Which was the right decision for everyone *but* her. It left a bitter taste in her mouth, because her dreams were precious to her, she'd fought so hard to attain them. But Santo was leaving her no other option. How could she fight him on every front?

Her head went back to the image of her son playing in the sand with Santo. The relationship they could have if he had a father who was in his life for every one of those moments versus the fragmented time he would have with him in a joint-custody arrangement. Leo could have everything she had never had. It was the thing that tipped the scale for her.

She might have made an unforgivable mistake in keeping Santo from his son, but she could rectify it now by doing the right thing. Even if it killed her to do it.

She swallowed past the lump in her throat that refused to produce the words that didn't seem to want to emerge. "All right," she finally breathed, "I will marry you."

Everything happened in a blur in the days after she'd agreed to marry Santo. Gia tried to take it one step at a time, to keep her world from spinning out from beneath her feet, but it was almost impossible with everything happening so fast it made her head whirl.

With the biggest launch in Supersonic's history on his hands and clearly not intending to let Leo out of his sight for even a moment, Santo took control of everything, including the logistics for their move back to New York, as well as for their wedding, which would be a private, civil ceremony held on the beach on Delilah's estate.

He was determined to see her named a Di Fiore before they returned to New York to protect her and Leo and, she suspected, to send a clear signal to her father that she and Leo belonged to him. And while the whole concept of *belonging* to Santo, belonging to any man ever again, stoked the anger that burned beneath the surface, she couldn't deny the necessity behind it.

She also couldn't deny the attraction a simple, private ceremony held after her big, glitzy wedding to Franco—an over-the-top occasion she had dreaded. Her mother, busy holding the family together in Las Vegas in her father's absence, the situation tense over whether he would testify in the hearings, thought it better they keep the ties severed between them until the political furor had died down. She was also, Gia could tell, concerned about the political ramifications of her return.

It hurt, because she missed her mother desperately. But she'd been doing this for two years now. She'd learned to separate herself from her emotions. What was a few more weeks?

Before she knew it, she was marrying Santo in a short, textbook ceremony on the beach with only Delilah, Desaray and Leo in attendance. The ceremony, conducted by a civil officiant, was over before it even seemed to begin. The brief, perfunctory kiss Santo brushed against her lips barely penetrated the ice-cold shell she had constructed around herself. It was the only way she knew how to cope, because the thought of what was ahead was terrifying.

Santo might have promised to protect her from her former life, but a collision with her father was assured. Her mother might have understood her struggles, have supported her decisions, but her father would not. He would be angry, *furious*. To him family, loyalty, was everything. And she had thrown that in his face.

Her head a circular storm of emotion, she refused to look back as they left for the airport and the private Di Fiore jet that was waiting. Leaving Delilah had been bad enough. Saying goodbye to the slice of paradise where she'd healed, where she'd become a different person, might break her.

The three-hour flight back to New York flew by as rapidly as everything else. Leo, who'd only been six months old when they'd left for the Bahamas, was beside himself with excitement in the luxurious confines of the jet, imagining himself a *supahero* on his way to a *mission*. Which was a welcome distraction for Gia, because with each mile the plane ate up toward the past she'd vowed to leave behind, the faster her icy calm faded.

New York was home, where she'd spent her entire life before she'd married Franco and moved to Las Vegas. But she had become a different person—strong and resilient—and she was fiercely protective of this new version of herself. She worried that by walking back into her old life, exposing herself to those influences, she'd become *that* Gia again. And that could never happen.

Soon, they were landing at a tiny, private airport in New Jersey on a spectacular mid-May evening. Benecio, Santo's driver, who'd had the foresight to install a car seat in the Bentley, was waiting for them. Leo, agog at Benecio's shaved head and ex-military presence, which oozed from every inch of his dark, perfectly tailored suit, soon found the skyscrapers of New York his next big distraction. He absorbed them with big eyes until he passed out halfway to Santo's Fifth Avenue penthouse, which left Gia to take in the pulsing energy of the city. The honking horns and endless cacophony of sound, which was complete sensory overload after her life in paradise.

Santo's five-thousand-square-foot duplex penthouse that fronted Central Park was unspeakably gorgeous, with its private wraparound terrace and infinity pool that offered breath-taking, panoramic views of the skyline. The double-height ceilings in the modern glass-and-gunmetal-inspired living room were spectacular, as was the art wall wine display and the sweeping metal circular staircase.

Santo, a fast-asleep Leo sprawled over his shoulder, intercepted the wary look Gia gave her surroundings as they climbed the stairs to the upper floor. "This clearly isn't going to work for us," he acknowledged. "I'll have my real-estate agent look for something else. Nico and Chloe bought in Westchester. Maybe that's something we'd want to consider. Or the Hamptons. I'd love to get out of the city."

Her stomach dropped at the speed at which it was all moving. But staying here would not be an option, Santo was right about that. She wouldn't be able to take her eyes off Leo for a second, or he'd be swooping down that sweeping banister. The pool, however, might be the perfect antidote for not having the sea at his doorstep, which Leo would surely miss.

Santo showed her to the beautiful blue bedroom his housekeeper, Felicia, had prepared for Leo. It held none of the adventurous boyish charm his bedroom in Nassau had. It was all smooth, perfectly designed angles, but the collection of stuffed animals they'd sent along ahead, arranged in a decorative pile in the middle of the queen-sized bed, would hopefully be enough to keep him from feeling too homesick for now.

She roused her son briefly to slip on his pajamas, then tucked him into the center of the big bed. She left the lamp on in case he woke, frightened in a strange place, then followed Santo on a tour of the upper level, which included the beautiful master suite. Done in more of those browns, creams and greys, and featuring another jaw-dropping panoramic view, it was overtly masculine. A sultan's den of pleasure with its massive mahogany four-poster bed, working fireplace and skylight that showcased the stars.

She could only imagine how many women Santo had entertained here. She pushed that thought out of her head and considered the rest of the room. The palatial walk-in closet, with its full dressing room, already contained her clothes, which Felicia had unpacked. The bathroom, almost like a spa, was glorious, as was the chandelier that sparkled in the ceiling—a decadent touch she had a feeling Santo hadn't chosen. It was all so beautiful, even her critical eye couldn't find fault with it.

"Why don't you relax?" he suggested. "Get settled in. I have a few emails to address before I join you."

*For what?* Her stomach swooped at the question, but she forced herself to nod. He'd been business-like ever since she'd agreed to marry him. Throughout the ceremony today, when he'd barely touched her. When he'd followed her wedding band with a magnificent, oval-shaped diamond that had stolen her breath.

Which had hurt, because whenever her life had gone sideways, Santo had been the one she'd run to. The person who'd made it all better. This time, however, she'd been the one to break them. Who'd crossed the line they'd so clearly delineated in their relationship that night and smashed a decade-long friendship she'd regarded as sacrosanct, only to replace it with something far scarier and far more powerful.

And maybe, she conceded, kicking off her shoes, that was another reason why she'd walked away from him that morning. Because she hadn't known how to handle what she'd unleashed.

Which left her with the question of what he expected of her tonight. The sparkle of the chandelier drew her eye to the gorgeous diamond glittering on her finger. She was his *wife*. Would he expect her to share his bed tonight? It made her brain blank to even think about repeating the devastating intimacy they'd once shared. But

Santo had made it clear he expected this marriage to be real in *every sense of the word.*

Rather than face that daunting prospect, she ran a bath instead. Enveloped herself in lavender-scented bubbles in the luxurious tub, with its spectacular view of Manhattan. Which only gave her more time to *think.*

She leaned her head back. Found herself spiraling into a place she rarely let herself go. Her marriage to Franco had been the most painful years of her life. She had blocked out much of it, because by the end, it had been a disaster, but now the memories came flooding back.

If she'd found it difficult to be a Castiglione, she'd found it even harder to be a Lombardi. Franco had been aloof and hard to know, exactly as her father had been. Angry at her for what she'd done, he'd been cold until after Leo had been born. He had allowed her to do a couple of decorating jobs on his hotels to keep herself busy.

She'd had good taste and he'd appreciated it. It had led her to believe that their marriage could work. That once they'd had their own children, when they had a family together, they could forge a connection between them. But that had never happened.

She'd been so intimidated by him, had never been comfortable with him. It seemed the harder she'd tried to conceive a child, the more difficult it had become, until her husband's jealousy of Santo had become a living, breathing entity that had driven an impenetrable wedge between them.

She hadn't blamed Franco. Had known the whole situation was her fault. But her husband's cruel, careless comments about her inability to conceive, about her failures as a woman and wife, had cut deep. He'd taken a mistress, which had almost been a relief for the reprieve it had been. But he had also insisted she stop working so that she could focus on a family. Provide him with an heir. Which had only made her feel more trapped and isolated than ever.

She'd hosted his dinner parties, stayed out of his business, did everything she was supposed to do. But each day the gulf had been driven wider between them, until her husband's death had mercifully ended a marriage that had been barely limping along.

She stared out at the skyline, the lights of the

city blinking like teardrops suspended from the tall, imposing skyscrapers. Perhaps it was true that her feelings for Santo had destroyed her marriage. But now that she'd broken *them* with her actions, she had no idea what they were. What they could ever be.

She felt utterly and completely lost.

Santo nursed a brandy in his study as a hushed blanket of black slipped over Manhattan. He'd called his brothers to let them know he was back. Dispensed with the dozens of emails that had filled his inbox during the flight home.

He should join Gia. Get some sleep before the insane day he had ahead. But he hung on a moment longer to finish the drink. To process everything in his head. And maybe, there was a little avoidance thrown in there, too.

He'd come back to New York a married man with a three-year-old son he hadn't known about. His life as he'd known it had been annihilated. He should be having some sort of an extreme reaction to it. Withdrawal from his bachelor life. Instead, he was numb, Lazzero's assessment of he and Gia from that night in Nassau running through his head.

*You've gone on a tear through half the women on the planet since her, but you're not even remotely interested in any of them... You are completely distracted.*

He wasn't actually sure that was true. He'd had a list of the attributes in the woman he'd been looking for. Abigail, the last serious candidate for a permanent role in his life, had lacked the fire and passion he was looking for, despite the heavy dose of altruism she'd possessed. Katy, the massage therapist who'd been so amazing with her hands in bed, had bored him out of it. Suzanne, the one before Abigail, had been both smart and sexy, but her promotion to assistant district attorney for the State of New York had called an abrupt ending to their relationship.

It was the one thing he wouldn't compromise on—a wife who wanted the same things out of life as he did. Who wanted to build the strong, impenetrable bonds of family that he did. Who was content to be at home, taking care of their child, putting her family first. Everything he'd never had.

He took a swig of the brandy, the aged malt burning a fiery path down his throat. In his defense, none of those women had been right. But to Lazzero's point, maybe the problem had always been Gia. That once, he'd thought she'd been *the one*. His soul mate. Only to have her shatter those illusions when she'd left.

At eighteen, he'd been no match for Stefano Castiglione. Gia had belonged to someone else. She was not *his*. It was a refrain he'd repeated to himself a dozen times over in the ensuing years. It was better, *easier* that way. Which had been the way he'd been content to play it until she'd crossed the elevator on that stormy night four years ago, blown his brains out with her innocence and passion, and he'd made the conscious decision to claim her as his.

He'd woken up the next morning, intent on speaking to her father. On taking her away from that life. On building a future with her. Instead, she had walked away from him and married Franco Lombardi without a backward look. Slammed the door on everything they had shared.

It had taken him months to blank the image of her with Franco from his head. To convince himself that she was just as emotionally damaged as his mother had been, just as unsure of what she wanted, and he was better off without her. And once he'd finally managed to put the memory to rest, he'd vowed she was a piece of his history never to be repeated.

His fingers tightened around the glass. So what the hell had he just done?

*The necessary*, a voice in his head responded. His marriage to Gia had been *necessary*. To secure his wife and son. To protect them as he'd promised.

So now, he acknowledged, downing the last sip of brandy, he was going to do just that. With his expectations firmly in place when it came to his wife, and fully aware of what she was and what she was not, he was going to put his relationship with Gia back on the rational, pragmatic plane he had promised himself. Piece together this family he'd been given and somehow make it work.

Dispensing with the tumbler in the kitchen, he made his way upstairs. His wife had taken a bath and changed into some filmy cream concoction that wasn't overtly sexy, with its silky, delicate material that flowed to her knees. It was the body beneath it that claimed his attention. He knew how perfect it was. The curve of her hips that filled the palms of his hands. How those curves nipped in to a tiny waist, then up to the voluptuous fullness of her breasts, with their feminine, dusky rose tips.

It was an image that would be imprinted in his head forever. Which didn't help him now as he lifted his gaze to her beautiful face, the lush fullness of her mouth, those emotive green eyes that made his body harden with predictable effect.

So he was hot for his wife. Wasn't that a good thing when this was *forever*?

The bath had dissipated some of Gia's tension, but she found her nerves ramping up all over again with Santo's reappearance in the bedroom.

His shirt sleeves rolled up in that sexy look he did so effortlessly, his shirt open at the collar to reveal hard, bronzed flesh, he was familiar, yet foreign, a new thickness and maturity to all that muscle she'd once known intimately.

The storm of mixed emotions coursing through her reached new heights, an inescapable awareness of him climbing up her throat. Which was not necessarily helped by the slow slide of his dark gaze as it worked its way from the tip of her head down to her toes, lingering on the fullness of her mouth, the swell of her breasts and the curve of her hip.

The aloofness he'd been wearing all day vaporized, replaced by a flare of heat that stole her breath. "How was your bath?" he murmured, keeping that whiskey-dark gaze on hers.

"Relaxing." She curled her fingers tight by her sides. "Did you get your work done?"

"Yes." He threw his phone on the table. "I have an early meeting in the morning. It's a quiet week on the social front, which is good because it will give you some time to get settled in. Benecio will be at your disposal. You will take him with you whenever you leave the apartment," he said emphatically.

A surge of frustration swept through her. "So it's back to me being a prisoner in my own life?"

"I wouldn't look at it that way," he countered smoothly. "Whether it's because you are a Castiglione or because you are my wife, Gia, you are a target. As is Leo. It is a reality you need to face."

Which she wouldn't have needed if she was still in the Bahamas. A wet heat stung the back of her eyes. Blinking it back, she snatched a short, silk robe from the wardrobe and shrugged it on. Santo covered the distance between them, his slow, purposeful stride accelerating her pulse. Stopping in front of her, he stuck a hand against the frame of the dressing room door and blocked her exit when she would have stalked out.

His deliciously enticing aftershave worked its way into her head as she sank back against the wall, a heady combination of bergamot and lime infiltrating her senses. His tall muscular body blanketing her with a wicked heat, she focused her gaze on a place somewhere in the middle of his chest.

Long fingers crawled up her nape, slid into her hair to tilt up her chin. He studied her face with such a thorough appraisal, she felt utterly transparent. As if he could see how desperately she was melting inside. "What's wrong, Gia?"

Frustration and fear and something else she was afraid to identify, something far more dangerous, bubbled up inside of her. "I am off balance, Santo. *Lost.* You've torn me away from a life I loved. Put me right back in the middle of this," she said, waving a hand toward the window and its unparalleled view of Manhattan.

"Am I simply supposed to walk back into everything that I was as if nothing has changed?"

"No," he said evenly, "you need time to acclimatize. To establish a new life for yourself, which will be built around the family we create together."

Her heart gave a bittersweet twinge. And what was that going to look like? She couldn't see her mother right now, the one person who would have grounded her other than Delilah. The Di Fiores were hardly likely to be any more welcoming. She'd taken Santo's son and run. Had deprived him of three years of his life. She couldn't imagine they would understand.

And then there was her father, and the looming question of Leo. The political time bomb she carried.

She expelled a breath. Leaned back against the wall. "What happens when my father resurfaces? He's going to hit the roof when he finds out what I've done."

His expression hardened into one of pure determination. "I told you I will handle your father. Leave him to me."

"*How?* How are you going to handle him? He

isn't simply going to play nicely because you ask him to, Santo. You know what he is."

"You don't need to know." His delivery was flat. Icy cool. "I know exactly who and what your father is, Gia. I will deal with him. What *you* need to focus on is settling you and Leo into a new life. Getting your bearings back."

She shot him a deadly look. "I am not a china doll."

"Clearly not," he said softly. "You took your child and walked away from one of the most powerful organized-crime families in the world. That took guts. But now it's time to relinquish control and let me handle this."

She inhaled a shaky breath. She wanted to do just that. Wanted to let him fix this as he'd fixed everything else in the past. But she felt so vulnerable, as if her soft underbelly had been exposed to the world again. And her father was a wild card no one could predict.

Santo ran a finger down the heated surface of her cheek, the slow caress rippling a reactionary path through her. "What else is going on in that head of yours?"

"I may have agreed to do this," she said huskily, "but that doesn't mean I am happy about it. You have turned my life upside down. Taken away everything I've built. I am angry with you. *Furious.*"

"Good," he murmured. "That makes two of us. We can work through that. But I need all your feelings out in the open where I can see them, Gia. I can work with that—the icy shell not so much. And as far as you being angry with me?" He tipped his head to the side. "Honor it, wallow in it if you need to, but you are going to have to get over it, because we *are* going to make this marriage work."

She swallowed hard, past the inevitability clogging her throat. His powerful length imparting a seductive heat, a faint darkness on his jaw where his stubble was beginning to show, the thick fringe of lashes over those beautiful mahogany eyes decadently tempting, he was far too close for comfort. Too close for her to think straight.

Her hands curled tighter at her sides. "I thought I would sleep with Leo tonight," she blurted out. "It's a strange place. He might get frightened."

His gaze drifted over the heightened color in her cheeks. The accelerated beat of her pulse at the base of her throat. "I think that's a good idea," he said quietly, lifting his gaze back up to hers. "Sleep with him for a few nights—he might need the comfort. But just to be clear, I am not okay with the concept of separate beds because I think it creates a distance between us before we've even started. And since I intend for us to start this relationship off on the right foot, that means we share a bed together, sex or no sex. We build an intimacy between us, which includes *you* opening up and sharing those thoughts and fears of yours."

The very concept of it made her brain freeze. She slicked her tongue over her lips in a nervous movement, Franco's appraisal of her as "ice-cold" and "not worth the effort" filling her head. "I'm not sure I can do that."

"You can," he rejected flatly. "You merely choose not to. You'd prefer to live in that safe, self-protective world of yours that has shielded you from real life as long as I've known you. It's how you've survived. But that isn't going to work for us."

She absorbed his utter implacability with a sinking heart. "Even if I can learn to open up, it's not going to happen overnight."

"I'm not asking for you to do it overnight. I'm

merely telling you there is no more running and there is no more hiding. There is only going to be the truth between us, Gia, so get that through your head."

# CHAPTER FIVE

GIA DID HER best to acclimatize to her new life over the next few days. A stunningly warm early summer heat blanketed the city as temperatures soared into the high eighties. She and Leo put on shorts and played in the park under Benecio's watchful eye while Santo worked, the two of them indulging in an afternoon ritual of ice cream and a dip in the spectacular terrace pool at the penthouse.

It was New York at its most glorious, the city transformed into a glittering, vibrant green jewel. It had an energy about it, an aura of excitement that Leo loved, regarding it all as a big adventure. But Gia missed the peace and tranquility of the islands. The simplicity of her life there. The job she'd loved so much. Her *freedom*. It was like a punch to the gut every time she thought about it.

Not to mention the fact that she was still so angry at Santo for taking it away from her, it was hard to find the peace she was looking for. She knew he was right—that she had to get over it if they were going to make this marriage work. But she *wanted* to wallow in it, to mourn what she'd lost, because it had meant everything to her to have that independence she'd fought so hard for.

And overshadowing it all was the news coverage of her father's flight from justice. The papers were positioning it as a glamorous international intrigue—a tangle between two foreign governments. Her father, through his lawyer, insisted it was all a tactic on the US government's part to expose holdings they imagined he had, but in reality, he did not. High drama played out for all to see.

It made her worry about her mother. How she was handling all of this. She was tough, she knew, because she'd had to be. She would have her family around her. But that didn't mean she wouldn't be reeling from it, her foundation rocked.

Meanwhile, in the shadow of it all, she was having dinner with the Di Fiore clan that evening, an event that didn't ease her nerves. She had grown up with Nico and Lazzero. Had known them since they were teenagers. But this was different. She was afraid they wouldn't understand the decisions she'd made when it came to Leo, exactly as Santo hadn't.

She had tried on and discarded five outfits before Santo came home from work. Standing in front of the mirror in the dressing room scrutinizing her latest choice—a turquoise, off-the-shoulder dress with a ruffle at the hem—she heard him blow through the front door of the penthouse.

Leo's excited greeting as he went running to meet him did something strange to her heart. If anything had felt right in all of this, it was the decision she'd made when it came to her son.

Every night, bar none, Santo had come home from work in time to have dinner as a family, then put Leo to bed, after which he would work until midnight with his grueling schedule. He was clearly committed to being the father his own hadn't, as Leone Di Fiore had been so caught up in his high-powered Wall Street career in the early years, then later in the bottom of a bottle, Santo had only a few distant memories of the bond they'd once shared. It made her heart hurt to think of it. To watch him changing history.

Her husband breezed into the dressing room, having left Leo to his collection of NYC first-responder toy vehicles he'd come home with last night, much to her son's delight. Dressed in a sharp navy suit with a pale yellow tie, with tawny blond stubble darkening his jaw, he looked so gorgeous he made her heart stutter in her chest.

She imagined the women of New York had spent the day watching him walk down the street drooling in his wake. And that was without the look he lavished on her, his dark, appreciative gaze taking in the flirty line of her short, feminine dress.

"You look amazing," he murmured, bending to brush a kiss against her cheek. "I only need five minutes to get out of this monkey suit. It's far too hot for this."

Which was such a shame, she opined silently, more than a bit off balance at the sight of him. Santo stepped back and stuck his fingers into the knot of his tie. "How was your day?"

She gave as casual a shrug as she could manage. "The same. The park. Ice cream. The pool. I'm exhausted. So is Benecio."

His mouth quirked. "Maybe we should switch. *I* sat through four hours of meetings this morning, spent my lunch debating our social-media strategy after one of our athletes decided to blow up Twitter by sending nude pictures to his girlfriend that were somehow leaked. Then," he continued, stripping off the tie and dropping it on a chair, "the icing on the cake was my afternoon spent ironing out a manufacturing flaw with the Elevate design team. *Not* what I needed at this stage of the game."

"Did you get it figured out?"

He lifted a brow. "The nude tornado or the potentially crippling flaw?"

"Both."

"Yes." He threw her one of those sexy smiles that could melt a woman's knees as he made quick work of the buttons on his shirt. The smooth expanse of rippling, bronzed flesh he exposed made her stomach contract.

"I will want my career back," she murmured, as a distraction more than anything else. "When Leo gets settled. I can only wander aimlessly around Central Park and eat ice cream for so long."

"Of course," he agreed smoothly. "But there's no hurry. Meanwhile, you can focus on *us*."

On the fact that he was now stripping off his dark trousers, revealing snug-fitting black boxers that left little to the imagination. Which brought every second, every minute of that explosive night they'd spent together, roaring back with crystal clarity. Because she remembered how amazing he looked. How *virile*. How incomparable. It was not what her strung-out nerves needed at the moment.

*Dear God.* She fumbled around for earrings to wear. Found some simple diamond teardrops that would enhance the feminine lines of the dress.

True to his word, Santo had given her the space she'd asked for. She'd been sleeping with Leo ever since that first night they'd come back, avoiding these kinds of intimacies. But sooner or later she was going to have to address what was between her and Santo.

Clad now in a pair of dark jeans and a black T-shirt that looked just as deadly on him as the suit had, clinging to his lean, hard body in all the right places, he propped himself against the dressing table, eyes on her. "You're nervous."

"A bit." She refused to show just *how* nervous she was.

"Don't be. You know Nico and Lazzero and you've met Chloe a few times. Chiara," he added, "is amazing. You'll love her."

She sank her teeth into her lip. "What do they know about us? About Leo?"

"The truth. That I have a three-year-old son with you and that we are married. All they need to know. Nico and Chloe are thrilled that Jack will have a playmate."

Which she had denied him for the past couple of years. A whirlwind of conflicting emotions sweeping through her, she presented her back to Santo so that he could do up the top clasp of her dress. They weren't helped by his close proximity, which only got worse when his fingers, having deftly dispensed with the tiny hook and eye closure, trailed a path down her spine to her waist, sensitizing every centimeter of flesh he touched.

Her bare thighs brushed against the rough denim that encased his length and his palms heated her skin, making her awareness of him sky-high—it was sensory overload. "Stop thinking about the past," he said softly. "Think about the *now*, Gia. The *right* decisions we are making. About this fresh start we have."

Her skin fizzled beneath his touch, a golden heat invading her blood. Her eyes fixed on his in the mirror, a luminous green snagging a slumberous black. She couldn't deny how tempting the thought was to believe that they could make this work. That somewhere in the midst of all of this insanity, of the mistakes she had made, of the gulf that now stretched between them, something good could emerge.

But there was also fear. Fear that clawed at her insides at making herself that vulnerable ever again.

He bent his head and pressed a kiss to the delicate skin of her neck. An involuntary shiver raked through her. She moved closer in an instinctive reaction. His hands dropped lower on her hips to hold her more firmly against him. More of those fleeting, butterfly-light kisses pressed down the length of her throat until it felt as if her skin was on fire.

He tightened his hands around her hips and turned her around. Gia sank back against the dressing table. Her pulse a frantic, staccato beat at her throat she couldn't seem to control, she read the dark intent in his gaze before he lowered his head to hers. A mad anticipation fizzled through her, sizzling her blood, just before a tiny, dark-haired dynamo launched himself between them.

"Wee-oh, wee-oh," cried Leo, waving his fire truck in the air.

The heat in Santo's eyes cooled, replaced by a reluctant amusement. "The very epitome of an inopportune moment," he drawled. "One we will pick up later."

He bent to scoop his son off the floor. Her cheeks scarlet, her head a muddled mess, Gia went and looked for her shoes rather than let her mind go down that path.

Nico and Chloe's Westchester estate sat on the banks of the Hudson, the magnificent Georgian home sparkling in the late afternoon sun. Situated on three acres of lush, picturesque landscape, it offered unparalleled privacy and endless vistas across the water. Private gates opened to the main residence, which was surrounded by multiple stone terraces and an in-ground pool.

It took Leo about five minutes to warm up to his new cousin, Jack, a gorgeous little dark-haired boy with a big personality, before her son was off and running, Jack's nanny in tow. Which was a bit unnerving, because deprived of her son's lively presence, Gia felt completely under the microscope.

Chloe and Chiara were amazing—warm and wonderful. Nico and Lazzero, on the other hand, were guarded with her. Polite, but distinctly cool. Particularly the aloof, hard-to-know Lazzero. Which wasn't entirely unexpected. The three brothers had always been close, given the way their family had shattered apart. It would take time to earn back their trust.

A hand fisted her chest. But hadn't that always been the way? Guilty until proven inno-cent? Never had anyone given her the benefit of the doubt—she'd had to earn it every single time. *Prove herself.* This would be no different.

She pushed back her shoulders and absorbed their scrutiny with an unflinching look. Chloe, quiet and lovely, soon took her under her wing, suggesting she and Chiara join her for a glass of wine on the deck while the men threw a football around with the boys.

A brilliant scientist who'd developed some of the world's most popular perfumes at Evolution, the cosmetics company she ran with Nico, Chloe told them about the new fragrance she was debuting at the Met Young Patrons party, one of the biggest nights of the year. It would go into all the gift bags for the influencers in attendance, but she'd send Gia home with a bottle of it tonight to try.

Chiara, a talented, up-and-coming clothing designer, was the polar opposite of Chloe. Stunning with her dark Latina looks and fiery personality, Gia could understand why the impossible-to-catch Lazzero had fallen for her.

Alight with the news that her hip line of street clothing, which had been garnering so much attention among the city's fashionistas, had just been picked up by one of the largest department stores in the city, Chiara was brimming with excitement.

"I am dressing a few people for the Met party," she buzzed. "Speaking of which," she said, tipping her glass at Gia, "Abigail Wright is going to flip her lid when she hears Santo is married.

Just last week she was telling me she is *not* over him. That she's only dating Carl O'Brien, the quarterback of the Stars, to make him jealous."

*Abigail Wright*. Gia's brain sifted through a mental list of who was who. *Miss Arkansas*. Abigail Wright. The paragon of virtue she was sure she could never live up to. Who was apparently dating New York's most famous quarterback.

"Half of New York's female population is undoubtedly in mourning," Chloe interjected drily. "No surprises there."

"Not that I'm going to dress her anymore," Chiara amended hastily. "He never looked at her the way he looks at you, by the way. You have nothing to worry about."

Gia's lashes swept down. "What do you mean?"

"Like someone would have to walk through him to get to you. I've never seen him like that."

A flush warmed her cheeks. That had always been Santo's way. But in this case, it didn't mean anything other than he'd married her for his son and he was protecting his investment. Because he was determined to carve out that perfect family he'd promised himself.

"I think it's obvious why Santo and I married," she said quietly, aware these women were too smart and perceptive not to sense the truth. "We did it for Leo."

Chloe studied her for a long moment with that quiet scrutiny of hers. "Is it? I don't pretend to know what happened between you and Santo. Frankly, it's none of my business. But you know him as well as I do. The last thing he would do is commit himself to a marriage he doesn't want. He could have his pick of any woman on the planet. So clearly," she observed, "there is something there for him. Something he thinks can work."

Or, Gia countered silently, he was simply going to *make* it work because he had to.

Chloe's words, however, stuck with her as the lazy evening stretched on, a delicious dinner served on the terrace amidst a stunning, rose-red Westchester sunset. Maybe she was right. Santo seemed committed to making this relationship work. Maybe it was *her* that was the stumbling block. Maybe she had to let go of this anger. Believe everything he was saying. That she and Santo had a foundation to build this marriage of theirs on that could make it a success. That once, they'd shared something rare and special and maybe they could have it again.

When her husband suggested they should leave as the sky darkened to black, the sound of an army of cicadas filling the air, a current of anticipation fizzled her blood at the promise of what was to come. She made a quick trip upstairs with Chloe to get the bottle of perfume she'd promised, and was about to join the others at the front of the house when she remembered she'd left her wrap on a chair on the terrace. Winding her way through the house to the patio, she had set one foot through the open sliding glass doors, before the low pitch of Santo's voice froze her in her tracks.

"What the hell is wrong with you?"

"I am attempting to hold my tongue, that's what I'm doing." Lazzero's voice held a dark frown. "Your shotgun wedding has us all a bit shell-shocked, Santo. I'm simply attempting to process it all."

"Some kind of a friendly welcome might be nice."

"She is a *Castiglione*," his brother said, biting out the words. "Her father is the topic du jour of the newspapers. She is a political liability. Immersing yourself in this, taking Stefano Castiglione on, is madness with the biggest launch in our history right around the corner."

"She is the mother of my child," her husband growled back. "There was no question as to what I'd do. You would have done the same."

"No," his brother said deliberately, "I wouldn't have. I think it's a mistake. I think *she* is a mistake. I can hold my tongue on your private affairs, Santo, but do not ask me to tell you lies about how I feel."

"You don't know her." Santo's voice was low, resonant. "You are judging her based on the family she comes from, not for who she is."

"I am *judging* her based on what I saw every day for a decade. Her running to you every time she had a problem. You playing knight in shining armor. You're going to spend the rest of your life trying to keep a woman like that happy. Dealing with her *backstory.* And you never will."

Gia's heart splintered into pieces. Unable to bear hearing any more, she turned on her heel and retreated the way she'd come, tears stinging the back of her eyes.

It wasn't anything she hadn't heard before. It shouldn't cut so deeply. It was the last comment that did it, because she knew it was true. Santo had always been her shelter. Her rock. She'd always run to him when she'd needed someone. It was exactly what she'd been trying to rectify when she'd started her new life in the Bahamas. To learn how to stand on her own two feet. And now, she'd lost that, too.

# CHAPTER SIX

SANTO FOLLOWED GIA into the penthouse. He stripped off his watch and tossed it on the dresser in the bedroom, while she put Leo to bed, frustration seething through his bones. He'd been so sure they'd been making progress in this détente of theirs only to have her freeze up on him on the way home as if the temperature had been subzero instead of damn near balmy.

He absorbed the icy look on her face as she slipped into the bedroom, slid the clip from her hair and threw it on the dressing room table, her silky blond hair swinging against the delicate line of her jaw.

"What the hell is wrong with you?" He leaned a palm against the dresser. "Everyone was making an effort to make you feel comfortable tonight. We were good and then we were not."

"It's nothing," she said frostily. "I'm tired. I'm going to bed."

"Oh, no." He eliminated the prospect of that

happening, covering the distance between them with swift steps. "We are not doing this again. I've made it clear that isn't how our marriage is going to work."

She stared him down with belligerent heat. "It's nothing. You are barking up the wrong tree, Santo. I'm tired. I want to go to bed. That's all."

"Gia," he growled, "you can tell me what's wrong or we can stay here all night." He spread his hands wide. "Your choice. I'm *easy*."

She hiked up her chin. "I overheard you and Lazzero talking before we left. About what a mistake he thinks I am. A political liability."

*Maledizione*. He raked a hand through his hair. "You heard that?"

"I was coming back to get my sweater. I'd left it on the terrace."

He absorbed the cloud of hurt suffusing her eyes, his insides contracting. "It doesn't matter what Lazzero thinks," he said quietly. "This is our relationship, not his."

"Which he completely disapproves of. Both of your brothers do."

"So what?" He shrugged "I'm sorry you had to hear that. Lazzero is being... *Lazzero*. You know what my brothers are like. But that doesn't mean he is right. Which is exactly what I told him." He shook his head. "You have to stop worrying so much about what other people think and focus on *us*."

"How can I?" she bit out. "You haven't lived with the constant judgment like I have, Santo. You *saw* it growing up. It doesn't matter how hard I work to prove myself as something other than a Castiglione, I will always *be* a Castiglione."

"So you rise above it. Choose how you define yourself rather than let others do it for you. We've had this conversation dozens of times, Gia."

*Yes, they had.* And yet, every time it kept on happening.

He waved a hand at her. "You think I don't understand what it's like to live with a legacy? My father imploded in spectacular fashion, Gia. Thousands of people lost their jobs when his company failed. The analysts couldn't wait to savage the great Leone Di Fiore in the press. The golden boy of Wall Street's meteoric fall from grace. Lazzero and I have had to battle that legacy every step of the way. If we make a wrong move, they point to my father. When we succeed, they tell us we've risen too far, too fast. It is *always there*."

"You can't compare the two," she shot back. "Your father was an honorable man. My father is…" She stumbled to a halt, her cheeks blazing. "You know what he is."

"What?" he prompted quietly. "Why don't you just say it?"

"You *know* why."

"You aren't bound by those rules anymore. You walked away, remember?"

The storm in her eyes brewed darker. *"Fine,"* she said. "You want to get the elephant in the room out in the open? My father is a *criminal*, Santo. A monster in a slick suit. He rose to the top of the food chain by the exercise of extreme power and brutality. He has *blood* on his hands. Who knows how much?"

He stared at her, shocked into silence.

Her lashes lowered, brushing her cheeks. "People *assume* that I am guilty by association. How can I not be when I lived that life? When I *condoned* what he was?"

"You don't choose who your father is," he said evenly. "You were too young and too defenseless to make any sense of it, Gia. When you got older, when you could make those decisions for yourself, you left. You made your choice."

But she had been indelibly shaped by who she was, as he himself had pointed out in the Bahamas. Gia curled her arms tight around herself and paced to the window, everything she'd kept hidden inside of her for what seemed like forever bubbling to the surface. Pushing at the edges of her tightly held composure. The secrets, the memories, the *shame* of it all.

And suddenly, she needed to get it out before it ate her alive. Before it destroyed her even more than it already had.

"I didn't know what he was in the beginning," she said huskily, turning to lean a hip against the sill. "I was dazzled by him. I *loved* him. I thought he was larger than life. I would see him for a few minutes before bed every night. I would make sure I had a witty thing to tell him, something to make it worth his while. A funny joke I'd heard, a cool fact I'd collected from my *National Geographic Kids* magazine." Her mouth softened at the memory. "He would laugh and tell me how smart or funny I was. It seemed, in that moment, like it was the best thing I'd accomplished all day."

Her innocence about her father, she acknowledged, stomach twisting, had still been alive and well then.

"But soon," she continued, "the rumors started. My father was climbing the ranks—gaining power in the family. He was always working. Even more distant than he was before. I would hear the whispers at school about what he was, something a kid's parents had seen in the newspaper or on TV. I would go home and ask my mother if it was true. She would tell me that successful people like my father were a target for those types of stories and that I shouldn't believe any of it. Nor was I to talk about it."

"You never did," Santo observed. "Not even when I asked."

"I was bound by the *omerta*—the vow of silence we take. Talking about the business could land my father in jail. We could be forced to testify. Or worse," she added matter-of-factly, "it could be used against us."

She wrapped her arms tighter around herself as the memories enveloped her. "I didn't know *what* he was until the night before my thirteenth birthday. We'd finished dinner. Mamma had gone to her sister's. I was bored and lonely, angry I wasn't out socializing like every other kid I knew. My father always held these secret meetings in his library at night. I was desperately curious about them. So, I slipped into the secret compartment behind the library wall."

The memory was burned into her head, an indelible image she'd never forget. Her heart had been beating so loud in her ears she'd thought it might thunder right out of her chest. Her fingertips clutched the gnarled old oak shelves in a death grip as she listened through the gap in the wood. She'd been old enough to suspect that what everyone had said was true, but hoped it wasn't. Had been desperate to prove all the catty whispers wrong. Because, of course, it *couldn't* be true. Her father couldn't be *that*.

"My father was meeting with my Uncle Louis. Who wasn't my real uncle at all," she acknowledged, her mouth twisting. "He was my father's top lieutenant. His right-hand man.

"My father and Louis were talking about Giuliano Calendri, the famous jazz singer my father hung out with. Giuliano was refusing to play an engagement at one of my father's casinos." The knots in her stomach pulled tight. "My father told Louis that if Giuliano *couldn't find the time* to play his gig, he would ensure he never did another date on the east coast. Then, he would break his knees."

"So then you knew," Santo said softly.

"Yes." But it had felt as if she hadn't known *anything*, really. Because if her Uncle Louis wasn't her real uncle, what *was* true? Were the stories in the newspapers true? How much else had her father lied to her about? Was *anything* real in her world?

"I almost got away with it," she reminisced. "Until one of my father's security men found me slipping back into the house." A chill went up her spine as she recalled her father's violent rage. The sting of his fingers as he'd slapped her face so hard, her head snapped back. She'd been in shock. Her father was hard. Undeniably ruthless. But he had never hit her before.

"He lost it with me," she said, lifting her gaze to Santo's. "He hit me. Told me I was never to do it again. That I should *know my place.* I never," she said quietly, "gave him reason to do it again."

Santo watched her with an unblinking look. "So you turned yourself into a straight A student. Won every track competition you entered.

Did everything you could do to earn his approval, including marrying Franco. Walking away from what we had."

She lifted her chin, Lazzero's soul-destroying words slicing open jagged wounds inside of her. "It was never going to work, Santo. *That's* why I walked away. We both knew it. It's why we avoided the attraction between us."

"I ignored the attraction between us because you were promised to someone else," he qualified. "In case you have forgotten that pertinent fact. I was trying to be sensible for the both of us, Gia."

"And the fact that it was complicated, that *I* was complicated, never figured into it?"

The evasive look on his face cut a swath right through her. "It is inconsequential," he murmured. "Because we crossed that line and now we are here. *Together.* Stop trying to throw roadblocks between us."

A hot ball of hurt lodged itself beneath her ribs. At him for refusing to acknowledge the truth. Anger at herself for ever agreeing to a marriage she shouldn't have. For allowing herself to believe, even for a moment, that it could work, because she had never been, nor would she ever be, what he needed. Nor what he'd wanted.

She hiked her chin higher, refusing to show the pain and humiliation shredding her insides. "I am telling you the *truth* you refuse to admit. It wasn't going to work then, and it isn't going to work now."

Santo absorbed the hurt darkening his wife's big green eyes. Watched her shut herself down. It *had* been complicated. He had held himself back because of it. But he'd picked her up and carried her into that hotel room, anyway, because he'd thought it had been worth it. That *she* had been worth it. And it infuriated him that yet again, she was denying everything it had been.

He stalked across the room and came to a halt in front of her. "First of all," he murmured, tipping her chin up with his fingers, "*you* are the one who walked away, not me, Gia. It may have been complicated, but *I* thought it was worth it. Secondly," he qualified, "if you had stayed around long enough to hear the end of my conversation with Lazzero, you would have heard me say that he needs to open his eyes, because you are the strongest, most courageous woman

I know to have walked away from everything you knew to protect Leo like you did. I respect that, even if I haven't understood all of the decisions you've made."

Her eyes grew large, glittering pools of emerald green in the lamplight. "And finally," he concluded, "*for the record*, I don't give a damn what anyone else thinks about us. I only care what *we* think about us. What we make of this marriage. So how about we focus on that?"

Gia sucked in a breath.

He swept the pad of his thumb over the trembling line of her bottom lip. "What are you so scared of when it comes to us?" he murmured. "Because I think it has to do with more than this."

"Nothing," she muttered.

"Gia." His tone commanded an answer.

"We went from zero to a hundred in one night," she whispered, eyes on his. "I don't know how to handle it. How to put the pieces back together."

"So we slow it down. Learn each other all over again."

She stared at him as if she wasn't quite sure how to do that. He braced both of his palms on the window on either side of her. Shallow, fractured with anticipation, her breath sat frozen, trapped in her lungs as he lowered his head. Waited, his mouth just millimeters from hers until she made the first infinitesimal move—a tiny lift of her chin. Then he closed the almost imperceptible gap between them and claimed her mouth in a slow, gentle kiss.

Lazy, sensual, *magical*—it was so unlike Franco's impatient, rough caresses, it rocked her world. Wiped the memories clean from her head. She slid her fingers into his hair and kissed him back, a leisurely, mutual relearning of each other that affirmed everything they had once been. Real. *Right*.

Gauging her responses, reading the softening in her body, he took the kiss deeper. She tipped her head back, slid her fingers to his jaw and accepted his questing foray. The slow slide of his tongue against hers was stomach-clenchingly erotic. The remembrance of a taste once savored and never forgotten.

It filled the jagged, empty holes inside of her. Banished the loneliness she'd felt for so long.

Heat swept through her—surged to every inch

of her skin. Slowly, seductively, he made love to her mouth until she melted beneath him, her limbs lax as she plastered herself against the glass.

Santo lifted his mouth from hers and took her in. Cheeks aflame with color, her breathing erratic, she watched as he dropped his gaze to the erect peaks of her breasts, which jutted through the silk of her dress. Her pulse beat an erratic edge as he splayed a warm palm against her rib cage. Slid his hand up over the smooth expanse of skin covered by the silk until he found the pebbled peak that throbbed for him. Eyes on hers, he rubbed his thumb over the distended surface. Stroked the need higher.

"Santo," she whispered, arching into his touch.

"You like that?"

*"Yes."*

He transferred his attention to the other hard peak. Stroked it to erectness. The hot stillness that floated in the air between them and the electric tension that seized her throat were almost unbearable.

"You are so beautiful," he rasped, his mouth trailing a path of fire down her throat. "You make me lose my head."

He hit the ultrasensitive spot at the base of her throat. She gasped and arched her neck to give him better access. He took full advantage, nuzzling and exploring until she flattened her palms against the windows and surrendered completely.

He slid a finger underneath the strap of her dress and slipped it off her shoulder, revealing a full, rose-tipped breast. Cool air slid over her heated skin as he weighted her in his palm. Her stomach clenched at the look of lust on his face. Right before he took her inside the heat of his mouth.

The sweet, all-encompassing rush of pleasure almost took her to her knees. He slid a muscled leg between her thighs and brought her closer. He was hot, hard and male, and it excited her beyond belief.

She moved against him. Whimpered. "Santo…"

He slid the other strap off her shoulder and flicked his tongue over her nipple. Gave her what her husky plea hadn't been able to verbalize. Desperate, aching for him, she pushed into his touch. Absorbed his heady torture. Almost cried out when he stepped away. But it was only to move behind her to undo the clasp of her dress.

It hit the floor in a whisper of silk. She tensed then, exposed to his gaze, because not even the heat pulsing between them was enough to wipe away the cruel taunts Franco had tossed at her when the tension between them had risen to a fever pitch. When she had failed to live up to his expectations on every level.

*Ice-cold and not worth the effort.*

Santo's fingers tightened around her waist. "Forget about him," he growled, pressing a hot, open-mouthed kiss to the delicate skin of her neck. She melted at the hedonistic touch. At the sensual kisses he pressed against her back as he worked his way down her spine. As desperate and urgent as the last time between them had been, this time was slow and achingly sensual. He lit her up with those skillful hands of his. Made her achingly aware of every centimeter of flesh she possessed as he trailed a path of fire over the rounded curve of her bottom.

She lifted a foot for him as he divested her of a sexy, high shoe. Pressed a kiss to the delicate arch of her foot that made her toes curl. Then he reached for the other shoe and stripped her of that, too.

Heat shimmered through her insides as he turned her around with firm hands on her hips. On his knees, every magnificent, muscled inch of him at her disposal, she thought her heart might crash through her chest. Naked, except for the flimsy panties she had on, she should have felt self-conscious, as lacking as Franco had painted her as. Instead, all she could see was the desire in Santo's eyes. The electric connection they shared.

He cupped the back of her knee. Slid a palm up the soft skin of her thigh to the rounded curve of her buttock. Eyes on hers, he traced the smooth edge of her panties. Absorbed the shiver of reaction that chased through her. "I want to take these off," he murmured. "Can I?"

She nodded, a barely perceptible movement of her head because she couldn't breathe. He hooked his fingers into either side of the flimsy piece of silk, and stripped it off. Hands on his shoulders, her fingertips curling into hard, bunched-up muscle, she stepped out of them. He tossed the filmy material aside, then brought her closer.

"Santo," she murmured unsteadily as he pressed a kiss to the soft flesh of her upper thigh, "what are you doing?"

"Slowing things down," he said huskily. "All you have to do is relax and enjoy it."

She was not *relaxed.* She was ready to jump out of her skin because he hadn't done *this* that night. But she was also insanely turned on, her body hot and liquid as she reached for the window frame behind her and clutched it with both hands. Widening her stance with an insistent push of his palm against her thigh, she watched as Santo set his gaze on her most intimate flesh, as he parted her with gentle fingers and set his mouth to her.

Her body clenched hard at the first slide of his tongue against her silken warmth. Reverential, decadent, it washed over her in the most exquisite wave of pleasure she'd ever felt. Her legs shuddered beneath her, threatened to give way. Cupping her knee in his palm, Santo urged her leg over his shoulder and her fingers into his hair. And then, there was only the way he devoured her, *savored* her, in the most erotic, intimate way possible.

*Oh, my God.* She almost moaned with relief

when he picked her up and carried her to the bed. But the torture didn't end there. He followed her down, spread her thighs wide and sought out her slick warmth with his fingers.

Talented, skillful, his deliberate strokes made her crazy. She arched her hips and moaned his name. He added a second finger, the sensation of fullness so exquisitely good it made her gasp out loud.

"Santo. Please—"

He bent to kiss her, his mouth against hers as his thumb massaged the tight bundle of nerves at the center of her. "Let go," he murmured. "Come for me, Gia."

She arched her hips to take him deep as his devastating caresses unleashed a hot, shimmering pleasure that radiated out from her core. Stroking her with those amazing hands, he drew it out, wringing every last ounce of pleasure from her until she collapsed on the bed, her orgasm all-consuming and never-ending.

When she finally emerged from the haze of pleasure, she found Santo sitting back on his knees, watching her with hot, dark eyes. A wave of heat suffused her cheeks at how completely she'd let go. How utterly abandoned she'd been.

She slicked her tongue over desperately dry lips. Averted her gaze. Only to find her attention captured by the erection pushing against the zipper of his jeans.

"You going to do something about that?" he murmured.

Had they not just shared what they'd just shared, had they not bared everything to each other on that stormy night four years ago, she might have been frozen right there. Instead, her head filled with images of what he looked like— hot, hard and silky smooth. *Heavenly.* And the temptation was irresistible.

She pushed herself into a sitting position. Went up on her knees in front of him. Lip caught between her teeth, she ran her fingers over the hard bulge under the denim that covered him. Explored the rigid length of him from top to bottom.

He hissed in a breath. "Maybe this was a bad idea," he murmured. But he let her play. Slide his zipper down, draw him out and find him with her hands. Velvety soft, he was sleek power over steel. Stomach curlingly masculine.

His breath grew deeper as she caressed him, the taut muscles of his abs convulsing as she ran her fingers over him with a firmer touch. A rough sound leaving his throat, he pulled her hands from him, rolled off the bed and shucked the rest of his clothing, until he stood, in the flesh, exactly as she remembered him—a perfect canvas of lean muscle that was breathtaking in its perfection.

But it was the possessive look in his eyes that scorched through her. The *way* he looked at her. As if she was something special to him.

It warmed her from the inside out as he joined her on the bed, scooped her up with one arm and brought her down on top of him, cradling her against his chest. The long, languid kiss he stole melted her insides. Annihilated the last of her defenses. "I want to be inside of you," he murmured.

His arousal, thick and ridged, jutted against her abdomen. The scent of their lust was heavy and humid in the air, a seductive, hedonistic mix that drove everything from her head but the need to have him. She raised herself up, her palms on his rock-hard chest, captured him in her hands and, slowly, carefully, lowered herself onto him.

Thick and powerful, he filled her like nothing else had. She drew in a deep breath as she

absorbed the shock of his all-consuming possession. The first time between them there had
been a fleeting moment of pain, before there
had been pleasure. This time, it was all pleasure.
Buried deep inside of her, she could feel the
pulse of his heartbeat, a carnal kiss that echoed
deep in her soul.

His velvet dark eyes anchored her in the moment. "You destroy me," he murmured. "Every
single damn time, Gia."

Her heart pulsed at the admission. At the look
of raw, uncensored emotion on his face. It did
something to her to know that he wanted her this
much. That he *felt* as much as she did. Healed a
broken part of her she hadn't been sure would
ever mend after Franco.

"Gia," he rasped, his voice a rough caress. "I
need you to move, *cara. Now.*"

Emboldened by what they shared, by the want
written across his face, she leaned forward,
pushed his hands over his head and locked her
fingers with his. Then she started to move, each
stroke of his body inside of her raking across
her nerve endings.

He let her take control. She lifted herself off
him, then took him back inside of her, wriggling

her hips as she adjusted to his potent possession. A dark flush of color stained his cheekbones as she drew out the moment. Took him harder and deeper with every stroke until they were both gasping at the pure sensation of it.

He freed his hands. She let him, because she wanted him to take control. To give her that pleasure she knew was waiting for her. He cupped her bottom in his palms and angled her so that the tip of his erection rubbed against a tender, aching spot inside of her. She threw her head back and moaned, each skillful, deliberate thrust he administered stealing her breath. Nudging her closer to the edge.

"Santo—"

His hands bit into her flesh as he throbbed and thickened inside of her. Brought her down to meet his punishing lunges. Told her in a guttural voice how good she felt. How perfectly she took him. How much he wanted her.

Her heart thundered at the magnificence of him. His chest heaving with the force of his breath, perspiration dotting the hard planes of his face, his body radiating a blanket of heat, he was as far gone as she was.

Her release began deep in her core, sweeping through her, tightening her muscles around him. Santo captured her by the nape, his fingers biting into her flesh as he watched her shatter around him. It was the most erotic, intimate experience of her life. Terrifying in its intensity.

She lowered her head to his, fused their mouths together and rode him to his climax.

Santo lay awake, Gia curled against his chest, her silky blond hair spilling across his shoulder as a sliver of moonlight filtered through the room. His head too full to sleep, too many emotions chasing through his chest to settle, he stroked a palm down the satiny soft skin of her back. Over the delectable curve of her bottom.

She had taken him apart tonight. Dismantled him with her truths. It illuminated so much about her, made sense of so many of the puzzle pieces he'd held, but couldn't seem to reconstruct. Why she hid behind those impenetrable walls of hers. Why she had walked away from them four years ago. Because she'd been taught that trust was an illusion. That the only person she could trust was herself. So she'd taken her son and ran.

Which hadn't been helped by her marriage

to Lombardi if her reactions tonight were anything to go by, he concluded grimly. A place he wasn't about to let himself go, because it made him want to hit something.

He captured a lock of her hair in his fingers, rather than address the knot in his chest. Watched the moonlight play across its golden strands. The intensity of what they'd shared together replayed itself in his head. The *singularity* of it. Her particular combination of vulnerability and strength had always touched something deep inside of him. The loneliness that had always emanated from her. The sense that it was Gia against the world. Maybe because it mirrored a piece of himself.

*That* was why it had been so intense. It had been his protective edge talking—the one he'd never been able to dismantle when it came to her. That was the only place he was ever going to allow his emotions to go, because letting himself feel the things he once had for Gia wasn't going to happen. Not when she'd already shattered him once. Not when Stefano Castiglione would no doubt waltz back into town when he was ready to take on Washington—a land mine he couldn't ignore. Not when Lazzero had been absolutely right.

His future was on the line with Elevate. His attention needed to be fully on the business, ensuring this launch went off without a hitch, because one misstep could bring it all tumbling down around them.

Which meant preserving this bond he and Gia had built—smoothing out the rough waters of his marriage was paramount. Which he now thought might actually be possible. He had finally gotten inside her head. He was starting to understand what made his wife tick. Which was half the battle.

He could work with that.

## CHAPTER SEVEN

GIA WOKE TO the bright light of another gorgeous, sunny New York day streaming through the floor-to-ceiling windows of the penthouse. It was not, she recognized with a start, the guest bedroom she had been sleeping in with Leo. It was the master bedroom. *She was in Santo's bed.* And *they* had just spent a steamy, passionate night together.

Eyes widening at the height of the sun, she threw off the sheets, ready to dash out of bed and confront disaster with a Leo gone wild, then remembered it was Saturday, and he was already up. Somewhere in the early hours, Santo had murmured to her to sleep and had taken her son down for breakfast.

The apartment, however, was silent, bathed in a hushed, luxurious glow as the city bustled to life below. She collapsed back against the pillows, her pulse settling with the knowledge her son wasn't sailing down the circular banister like a real *supahero*.

She felt vulnerable, turned inside out after what she and Santo had shared. Full of emotions she didn't know how to process. The last time she'd felt like this, she'd run. She'd thrown away everything she and Santo had shared. Which had been a total disaster.

This time, however, she couldn't run. She had committed to this new life she was building with him. To making this marriage work. Which left her to wonder what it was, exactly, that she'd walked away from.

*It might have been complicated, but I thought it was worth it.*

She dug her teeth into her lip. Had she walked away from something amazing between her and Santo? Had she let her fears and insecurities destroy something that could have been everything she'd ever envisioned?

Her chest clenched into a fist. Secretly, desperately, in a part of her she'd refused to reveal, she'd wanted to be that girl on his arm. The one in the center of all that golden light. It had hurt to watch him move from one woman to the next, knowing she would never be the one. The one he chose, because she was who she was.

Had all of her assumptions been wrong?

She had thrown her worst at him last night. All of her secrets. Santo, however, had not flinched. Hadn't blinked. Had acted as if none of it had mattered. But what would happen when the news of his marriage to her became public knowledge? When she became that liability Lazzero had predicted? Because that part of what he'd said had been undeniably true.

Would Santo regret his decision then? It was hard to have faith he wouldn't, when every good thing she'd ever had in her life, every friendship, every fledgling bond she'd forged, had eventually been destroyed because of who and what she was. Could her relationship with Santo be any different?

Her thoughts were interrupted by the sound of voices, followed by an explosion of tiny limbs as her son launched himself into the bedroom and onto the bed. "Mamma," he cried, throwing his chubby arms around her. "We bought *bugels.*"

"Bagels," Santo corrected, strolling in behind her son, a coffee from her favorite bakery and a brown bag in his hands. "Of which your son had two, by the way. He clearly likes to eat as much as I do."

Which did not show on his lean, sculpted body, *at all*. Gia's pulse did a ridiculous jump at the sight of her husband in a baseball T-shirt and another pair of those dark denim jeans that hugged every delectable inch of him.

"Sleepyhead," Leo chastised, ruffling her hair. "Mamma tired?"

Santo's gaze met hers over her son's head, a dark glitter of amusement lighting its midnight depths. "Mamma had a busy night. She needed the sleep."

"Santo," she breathed, giving him a you-need-to-filter look.

"What?" Her husband deposited the items in his hands on the bedside table, braced a hand on the headboard and bent his head to hers to press a long, lingering kiss against her lips. "You were...*busy*."

Leo watched the whole thing with a huge smile on his face. "And if he repeats that to someone else?" she challenged.

"He will forget about it in about sixty seconds," her husband drawled. "His attention span is that of a gnat. He was a menace in New York traffic."

Her heart skipped a beat. "Relax," Santo murmured. "I had him glued to my side the entire time."

Leo tugged on his T-shirt. "Look," he said proudly. "They're the same."

She took in the T-shirt her son was wearing. It was an exact replica of the one her husband had on, albeit a third of the size. It did something strange to her heart to see the two of them dressed alike, the same, unmistakable blond cowlick rendering them equally handsome.

"You went shopping?" she asked.

Santo lifted a shoulder. "He saw the T-shirt in a window. It was a Supersonic design. Also," he added with satisfaction, "establishing the right loyalties is something that needs to start young. We had a conversation about Joe DiMaggio on the way back. Although," he conceded, "I was doing the most of the conversing. Leo was chasing a butterfly."

The lump in her throat grew to the size of Manhattan. Santo's gaze darkened as he read the emotion on her face. "You do, however," he murmured, tracing a thumb along the edge of her jaw, "have to get up. We have things to do."

She frowned. Snagged the coffee from the dresser. "It's Saturday," she said, taking a sip. "What do we have to do?"

"We're going house shopping. My agent gave me a call this morning. There's a property in Southampton that just came on the market. Ocean front. Amazing views. It won't last the day."

*Southampton.* It was one of her favorite places on earth, with its ethereal views and windswept beaches. *Heaven.* To buy a house there was her dream.

"Ocean," Leo echoed happily. "We need shovels."

Southampton, situated on the south-eastern end of Long Island's South Fork, had been home to famous family dynasties for over a decade. Its rugged beauty had attracted some of the great industry titans, New York's most influential financiers, as well as a who's who of the Manhattan social circuit. Alight with glamour in the height of the summer, the village was buzzing with flashy cars and designer outfits.

The house the agent showed them lived up to its billing. Located just a short walk from the village's trendy Main Street, with its high-end galleries, restaurants and shops, it sat at the end of a wide, tree-lined street, directly on the beach. A magnificent, traditional colonial-style Hamptons home, it had five bedrooms and a wraparound porch that offered up the most spectacular sunset views.

Gia adored its rugged ocean ambience, high-vaulted ceilings and massive fireplaces. It felt like a home even though it was clearly a show-piece, and it gave her a taste of the serenity she'd had in the Bahamas. Santo loved the beautifully manicured tennis courts, the expansive blue-stone patios and the waterside gunite pool. Leo, as predicted, tripped over himself gushing excitedly about the ocean and the boats.

"You love it," Santo observed, as they stood side by side on the terrace drinking in the view while the real estate agent showed Leo the beach.

"*You* love it," she countered. "You are drooling over those tennis courts."

"And the running trail along the water. It would be incredible in the morning. You would enjoy the view while I annihilate you."

The thought of running here in the morning with him, like they'd used to, exchanging the confidences they'd had, squeezed something tight in her chest. "You mean while *I* annihilate *you*."

"As I recall," he murmured, "you only did that once. And it was because I had a leg cramp."

Which was true. She hated that. But she did love the house.

They bought it, on the spot. Leo, thoroughly overexcited by the whole adventure, was drooping by the time they walked through the door that evening, having missed his afternoon nap. Santo carried him upstairs to his bedroom and set him down on the bed to change him into his pajamas, while Gia went on a search of his blue blanket.

"Want my bed," Leo pronounced as he lifted his arms for Santo to slide off his T-shirt.

"You are almost there," said Santo, slipping off the T-shirt. "*Supaheroes* need their suit, you know."

Leo's bottom lip quavered. "Want *my* bed."

Gia paused in her search for the blanket. She'd known this was coming—the moment when her son's new reality began to sink in. When he began to realize the big adventure was a permanent thing. When he started to miss everything that was familiar to him. But the desolate look on his face made her heart plummet to the floor.

"We live here now," Santo said gently. "Remember that blue room you saw today? It's going to be yours. We'll make it into a *supahero* hideout."

Leo shook his head. "Want *my* room. *Friends*. Want to go *home*."

Santo tried to comfort his son, but Leo was too overtired and too overwhelmed to see straight. A tear slid down his cheek, and he kicked his hands and feet, refusing to let Santo slide on his pajama bottoms. Gia scooped the blanket off the floor and moved swiftly to intercept, but it was too late. In the blink of an eye, her son descended into a full-scale meltdown, pummeling his fists against Santo's chest and demanding to go home.

She took Leo from her shell-shocked husband. Leo clutched his blanket, his sobs of "Mamma" dampening the fabric of her T-shirt. She sat down and pressed him to her chest, holding him tight.

"Leave him with me," she murmured to Santo. "It's been a big day."

* * *

Santo made himself an espresso in the kitchen, intent on returning a couple of urgent emails. The deadlines were piling up with the massive launch he had in front of him, so Saturday was no obstacle to the work that had to get done. But he was so thoroughly shaken by his son's temper tantrum, by the transformation of his earlier, sunny demeanor into the frightened, miserable boy upstairs, by his inability to comfort him, he was utterly distracted.

It sent him back to the day his own world had been pulled from beneath his feet. He'd been thirteen. His father barely *compos mentis* in the wake of the collapse of his life, his mother gone in its dissolute aftermath. He'd spent the next week wondering which bike to take with him to the tiny apartment they'd rented above the hardware store where Nico had gotten a job, while attempting to process the fact that his mother was gone for good this time.

Walking into that dingy apartment for the first time had shocked him. Unnerved him. Everything had felt foreign to him—the neighborhood, with its gritty, boarded-up feel, the cramped, two-bedroom space he and his family had crammed themselves into. There'd be no defense against his father's first bender in their new, so-called home that night. The buffer of his mother's protection, her only nod to a maternal instinct, was gone for good. His new reality a shock to the system.

He'd had a massive temper tantrum that first night, unable to cope with all the changes. At having to share a bedroom with Lazzero. At becoming a part-time caregiver to his father, an experience he'd found terrifying with the shell of a man his father had become. At the train he would now have to take to school. Before Nico had put a halt to it with a grim command to "suck it up" because they were going to make this work.

And maybe, he recalled, his insides shifting, that was what had frightened him the most. How his eldest brother, strong, stoic Nico, had looked as lost and displaced as he had.

His brothers had been consumed by their own internal battles. The bonds between them back then had been all about survival. The difference for Leo, he determined, drawing in a deep breath, was that his son would never grow up in an emotional vacuum. He would have all of the love and support Santo had never had. The rock-solid stability of his world going forward.

He leaned back in his chair, coffee cup in hand, eyes on the skyline spread out in front of his office window. He'd been so focused on doing what he thought was right, what he thought was best for his son, he hadn't fully considered the impact it would have on him. But clearly, he conceded, the knot inside of him twisting tighter, he should have considered it. Because hadn't he done to Leo exactly what had been done to him? Pulled his world out from beneath his feet? Stripped him of everything that was familiar to him?

Except Gia. His head went back to how trustingly his son had curled into her. She was his world. The constant in his life. She made all the difference.

What he needed to do, he concluded, was stay the course. Keep the promises he'd made.

Gia padded into his office a short while later and perched herself on the corner of his desk. He looked up from the report he'd been studying. "How is he?"

"He's asleep." Her mouth softened. "The last couple of weeks have been a lot for his little brain to absorb. He has one of those meltdowns every once in a blue moon."

Santo's stomach coiled. He never wanted to see his son like that again. *Ever.*

"He's fine," she murmured, lifting a hand to brush against his cheek. "What," she queried, a wry note in her voice, "is going on in that head of yours? You're in another world."

He pushed aside the complex ball of emotion winding his insides tight. Moved his gaze over her in an effort to distract, finding himself more than occupied by the white cotton T-shirt she had on with cherry-red shorts that barely skimmed her thighs.

She flushed under the heat of his gaze. "I wasn't talking about that."

"I am." He pulled her onto his lap with a tug of his fingers around the slim curve of her wrist. He acknowledged why no other woman had ever been enough for him as he absorbed the flare of fire in her beautiful eyes, the voluptuous perfection of her body that fit so easily in his arms. Because none of them had ever been *her.*

Rather than consider that discomforting thought, he slid his fingers up to her nape and brought her mouth down to his for a kiss that soothed the ache inside of him.

Gia spent the next couple of weeks taking care of the details on the Southampton house, working on a design for the breezy, contemporary great room she'd envisioned. It kept her busy while Santo worked like a mad man getting ready for his big launch, gone by six every morning, home just in time to have dinner with them and put Leo to bed.

Which meant the only real time she had with him were the nights. Stomach-clenchingly hot affairs in which they couldn't seem to get enough of each other. As if once unleashed, their hunger was unquenchable. Which wasn't helping with her vow to keep her feelings for him on an even keel.

He might have said he'd thought they'd been worth it, but that had been then and this was now. Even if he did learn to forgive her for what she'd done, she would be a fool to think he'd ever let himself feel the way he once had about her.

Distraction seemed preferable. Particularly when the Met Young Patrons party lay ahead. It was one of the city's most prestigious events, thrown every summer to fund its annual initiatives, and would mark her debut as Santo's wife. Her reintroduction to Manhattan society. It was like being thrown to the wolves all over again. But since Chloe, one of the museum's largest donors in her role as chairwoman of Evolution, was patroness of the event, skipping it was not a possibility.

It wasn't until the afternoon of the party that she discovered her dress for the event had somehow acquired a stain on the front of it. Clearly, her efforts at distraction had been a little *too* successful.

She hadn't done any socializing in Nassau. Her wardrobe was limited. And since she couldn't just pull something out of her closet in the hopes that it would work, Chiara, thank goodness, came to the rescue. Not only did she have impeccable, trendy fashion sense, but she also had a curvy figure just like Gia's.

With Leo safely installed with Chloe's nanny, Anna, for a sleepover with his cousin Jack, she and Chiara went to a tiny boutique owned by a friend of Chiara's on West Broadway. Her sister-in-law made it clear she didn't need to pick one of her own designs, but Gia immediately fell in love with a sultry, bohemian number from her collection. A rich shade of cream, its twisted neckline was done in a halter style, her favorite, with the front plunging to a wrap waist.

Dress in hand, she set off for the quirky, luxe fitting rooms to try it on. She presented herself for Chiara's inspection, taking in her reflection in the large horizontal mirrors in the lounge. "Is it too much?"

Chiara inspected her from top to bottom, a slow smile curving her lips. "It's just enough. The color is amazing with your skin."

"But this," Gia said, gesturing to the expanse of skin the keyhole effect bared, including the tiniest hint of the swell of her breasts. "I can't wear anything underneath it."

"That would be the point." Chiara's dark eyes sparkled. "It's sexy without being overt. Perfect. Santo will be picking his jaw up off the ground. *Trust me.*"

She did trust Chiara. Although she wasn't at all sure what she wanted Santo's reaction to be anymore. Her head was too muddled. So she bought the dress instead.

Now, if she could only get rid of her raging nerves about the night ahead.

\* \* \*

The Met Young Patrons party was hosted at The Cloisters, one of New York's hidden gems. The replica medieval monastery in Upper Manhattan, which housed the museum's superb collection of medieval art and architecture, was spectacular, harkening back to a different age.

Built in the 1930s by the American oil magnate John D. Rockefeller, to showcase the large collection of medieval art he'd recently acquired, then gifted to the Met, the Cloisters sat in a picturesque setting overlooking the Hudson River. All of the guests agreed it was worth the forty-minute trip from the center of the city as they made their way up the red carpet to the top of the steps, greeted by waiters carrying trays of champagne.

The main hall, where the cocktail hour was being held, was bathed in purple and pink light projections that cast the ancient artwork and stained glass windows in a luminous glow. For Gia, the dark atmosphere fit the tone of the night. Everyone who was anyone in Manhattan was in attendance tonight.

Some of the faces were familiar, some had changed. What hadn't evolved was Manhattan's predilection for gossip—the eternal, inexorable fuel it operated on. Santo was too high-profile a personality for there not to be talk about his sudden change in marital status. Which, of course, unearthed the subject of who she was and all the salacious gossip that surrounded her father.

It was the evening's tasty tidbit. She could see it in the sideways looks thrown her way. Hear it in the sly questions disguised as social niceties. She would have had to have been deaf, dumb and blind not to notice it. The difference from every other occasion in which she'd endured such speculation was that tonight, she had Santo by her side.

Lethally attractive in a silver-grey suit and a dark blue shirt, he curled his fingers around hers, his hawklike gaze never leaving her as they made the rounds of the affluent crowd. Which was helpful as they came face-to-face with a particularly notorious clique of women she'd known from school.

The three organizers of the evening had frozen her out in the past and they did so again tonight. A knot formed in her stomach as they fawned all over Chloe and Chiara, inviting them to join the committee they were chairing for the Central Park Conservatory, while ignoring her completely.

Her smile faltered, her carefully constructed exterior giving way beneath one too many knocks. Santo closed his fingers tighter around hers and murmured in her ear, "Tougher and stronger, remember?"

The low prompt took her back to another place and time. To the afternoon she'd found out that her father had strong-armed her coach into giving her a position on the track team at school. But she hadn't known that part.

It had been the best day of her life as she'd walked off the field confident in her win, cheeks flushed with victory, only to overhear two of the other girls talking about her father in the tunnel on the way to the locker rooms. How *unfair* it was.

She'd turned and walked in the opposite direction, tears burning her eyes. She'd thought she'd earned it. That, for once in her life, she hadn't been defined by who she was—she'd been judged by her performance on the field instead. Which had once again turned out to be an illusion, like everything else.

Santo, on the field for his football practice, had taken one look at her face and walked away from his scrimmage, which had nearly gotten him booted off the team. But instead of giving her the sympathy she'd expected, he'd shaken his head instead and told her that quitting wasn't an option. That she needed to be "tougher, stronger than all the rest. Prove herself better," because that was the only thing that would put the naysayers to rest.

So she had. She'd turned the other cheek. Trained harder, longer than all the rest. And recorded the fastest time for a female runner that year in the city championships.

She pushed her shoulders back as they moved on through the crowd. Lifted her chin. He was right. She was better than this. Stronger than this. She would not let them get to her.

Chiara, resplendent in a midnight blue beaded dress of her own creation and Chloe, elegant in white, ankle-length Roberto Cavalli, soon stole her away for a gossip as they enjoyed the atmospheric artwork. Gradually, enveloped by the warmth of the other two women, her stomach began to unfurl. She'd never had allies. *Friends.*

Women who would look out for her, other than Delilah. A *family* who would protect her. And now she clearly did.

Santo leaned a hip against the bar, keeping one eye on Gia while he caught up with Lazzero after his brother's trip to Europe. The most beautiful women in New York were in the room tonight, but none of them made his pulse accelerate like his wife did in the knee-length cream dress that plunged nearly to the waist. She had the most jaw-dropping legs he'd ever seen. Followed by every other part of her anatomy that had held him spellbound for weeks, with no sign of that particular affliction waning.

She had handled all the gossip tonight with a quiet dignity he was coming to expect from her. With that iron spine she'd acquired. She might be thrown, but she was holding her own. Glittering like the brightest jewel in the night. It was a sexy, empowering transformation he couldn't take his eyes off.

"Everything okay in paradise?"

He transferred his gaze to his brother. Ignored his mocking gibe just as he'd avoided every other conversation about his wife over the last couple of weeks, because then it would devolve into a debate about Stefano Castiglione and how he continued to dominate the headlines. Which was already enough of a distraction, quite frankly.

"Actually," he drawled, "it's perfect. Thanks for asking."

His personal life was exactly where he wanted it to be. He had a beautiful wife, an amazing sex life and a confident, happy son who made him smile at the end of every day. As close to perfection as it came.

"Good to hear." Lazzero tipped back a mouthful of Scotch. Pointed his glass at him. "I bumped into Gervasio Delgado in the airport in Madrid. We're having dinner with him on Saturday night."

Santo blinked. Gervasio Delgado, the Spanish retail czar, had reinvented the way fashion was delivered to the masses with his on-demand manufacturing model. He also commanded the world's most popular clothing store chain, Divertido.

He arched an eyebrow at his brother. "Delgado is a notorious introvert. How did you manage that?"

His brother shrugged. "He asked me what we

were up to. I told him about Elevate. His curiosity was piqued."

Santo's blood fizzled at the possibilities. "You think there's potential there?"

"He needs a shoe for the first wave of his spring campaign. It could be a massive win for us."

He got why Lazzero was tempering his enthusiasm. Gervasio Delgado was a passionate, creative personality whose whims changed with the wind. It could turn out to be nothing. Or everything.

"Delgado is bringing his wife," Lazzero continued. "Chiara almost fell off her chair when I told her who we're having dinner with. Which could be a problem," he observed, a wry note in his voice. "I might have to muzzle her. Gia, on the other hand, could be an asset. Delgado mentioned Alicia, his wife, is remodeling their house in Marbella. They can talk shop."

Which was perfect. His wife was a brilliant designer, the sketches she was putting together for the house in the Hamptons fantastic. She would be the perfect complement to Alicia Delgado. But right now, he allowed, all he wanted to do was take her home, strip that dress off her and avail himself of every inch of her beautiful body.

Dinner was served alfresco in the Cuxa Cloister Garden. It was a spectacular setting, mirrored banquets set alongside rose-pink marble columns, the candlelight flickering in the night as black-coated servers flitted here and there in an effort to get everything just right. By the time the elegant, sumptuous dinner had been served and Gia had consumed a couple of glasses of the delicious sparkling wine that accompanied it, she was feeling a bit light-headed.

Maybe it was the way Santo kept finding excuses to touch her. The hand he kept on her thigh throughout dinner, his warm palm burning a seductive brand into her skin. The looks he kept throwing her in between conversations. It was impossible to ignore the electricity that ran between them.

They moved back inside to enjoy the musical entertainment in the moody, spectacular Fuentidueña Chapel. Reconstructed from pieces of a Romanesque-era Spanish church, the lights of the chapel had been lowered to a mysterious blue to focus attention on the magnificent dome and its beautiful Byzantine frescoes.

"I think," Santo murmured, catching her hand in his, "we should dance."

She couldn't actually find any reason to object, except the thought of it made her palms go damp and her knees weak. In the dark blue shirt that stretched across the rippling muscle of his shoulders, his jacket somehow having been lost along the way, *he* was the thing stretching her nerves over tenterhooks. Which wasn't a reason she could actually verbalize, so she followed him to the packed dance floor instead.

They had almost made it there when they were intercepted by the stunningly beautiful Abigail Wright and her big, wide-shouldered, square-jawed quarterback, Carl O'Brien. A tawny-haired Southern belle with a heart-shaped face and sparkling blue eyes, Abigail was, quite literally, perfection. Her sexy drawl when she greeted Santo only added to her devastating charm.

"Good news travels fast," Abigail murmured, with a wounded look in her eyes she almost, but not quite, smothered. "Your PR team reached out to me last week to emcee the event in

Munich," she informed Santo. "I almost couldn't believe my ears when they told me the news. Congratulations."

Santo kissed her on both cheeks. "Thank you. And thank you for agreeing to do the event on such short notice. A conflict in schedules. I know they appreciate it. And you will be amazing. Carl," he said, turning to greet the quarterback, "good to see you. When are you going to come over from the dark side and join us?"

The quarterback, who was extremely handsome in a rough, rugged kind of way, gave a lazy shrug of his shoulder. "My contract is up next month. We were just about to renegotiate. I might be persuaded to switch if the offer is right."

Santo's eyes glittered with opportunity. "Good to know. We will talk."

They chatted about the youth leadership conference Supersonic was sponsoring in Munich in several weeks, the event Santo's PR team had asked Abigail to emcee, at which Santo was also apparently speaking. Which unearthed a curl of jealousy in Gia. He and Abigail would be in Germany together. Sharing a luxury hotel, no doubt. Perhaps an intimate dinner together?

The claws of jealousy sank deep. Abigail asked all the right questions about the event. It was the platform she'd built her winning state title on, after all—the future of today's youth as the driving force of global change. It was impressive. *She* was impressive.

Gia wanted to hate her, but found that she couldn't. Abigail was clearly a serious and passionate supporter of the cause she'd chosen to embrace. She would have been the perfect wife for Santo. They would have been the ultimate power couple. Taken Manhattan by storm. *Abigail* would not have been causing waves by her mere presence at Santo's side.

Her stomach sank to the floor. She tried to push aside her thoughts as the conversation ended and Santo led her onto the dance floor.

Santo, ever perceptive, tipped up her chin with his fingers. "What's wrong?"

"Nothing."

His mouth curved at the lone word, imbued with far more emotion than she'd intended. "You're jealous."

"She would have been the perfect wife for you, Santo."

"Perhaps on paper," he conceded. "She is

beautiful, talented and smart. She ticks all the boxes. But there was something missing."

"Which was?" It felt dangerous to ask the question. To expose more of herself to him. To find out what the breach in perfection had been, but she couldn't resist the need to know.

"Fire," he murmured, eyes on hers, "spark. Although," he added huskily, "I *like* that you are jealous, *cara*. That you *care*. It shows that you are invested in this relationship. That I am not the only one intent on making this work."

There was no hint of amusement in his gaze now, only a quiet message that the next step was hers as he tightened his fingers around hers and drew her close. She was terrified to let him in. Scared she was halfway to falling in love with him again. That maybe, she'd never stopped.

His palm spread against the small of her back to keep her from bumping into the other dancers in the packed space. They were close, his hard-packed body brushing against hers so she could feel every muscle and tendon of his powerful thighs pressed against hers. The faint abrasion of his stubble against her cheek.

Her pulse quickened as he slid a hand into her hair and tilted her face up to his. She felt the warm caress of his breath right before he claimed her mouth in a slow, deep kiss that was perfection. Everything faded to the background—the music, the other dancers, the spectacular setting—and each languorous slide of his mouth over hers pulled her deeper into the abyss.

She melted into him. Felt the thick, hard length of his arousal pressing against her thigh.

Her eyes flew open. Santo lifted his head to look at her, the potent sensual awareness that had been building between them all night exploding into flames that licked at his velvet, dark eyes.

"We are leaving."

They sought out the other Di Fiores to say goodnight. Gia made a quick trip to the powder room while Santo filled in Lazzero on the opportunity with Carl O'Brien. She had repaired her lipstick and powdered her nose and was on her way through the main hall, walking toward the exit to meet Santo, when a voice hailed her from behind.

She turned to find Nina Ferrone, a hotelier who owned several boutique properties in the city, bearing down on her like the dynamic force of nature that she was. A sophisticated blonde in her early fifties, she was covered from head to toe in designer couture.

"I'm so glad I caught you." Nina brushed a brisk kiss to both of her cheeks. "I saw you earlier, but I couldn't get across the room. You know how these things are."

She introduced her daughter, who'd accompanied her to the event, then got straight to business. "Delilah mentioned you were back in New York. I need some help freshening up The Billiards Room on the Upper East Side. Delilah mentioned you'd done the work on the Rothchild Nassau I loved. Would you be interested in doing the work on The Billiards Room for me?"

Gia's heart jumped. The Billiards Room was one of Manhattan's funkiest, most exclusive hotels. It had a fantastic Regency vibe to it that transported you back to another time and place, complete with a gorgeous, hand-carved wood library Nina had brought over from England. She had always loved the place. But New York was New York and Nina would likely want the work done yesterday.

She swallowed back a pang of regret. "I don't

think I can do it. My son, Leo, is only three. He takes priority. I had a very flexible work schedule with Delilah."

"She mentioned that." Nina shrugged a shoulder. "It isn't a job I can give to just anyone. It has to be the right fit. Delilah says your work is flawless. I'm happy to be flexible with your schedule, my only stipulation being," she qualified, "that the work needs to be done by the spring. I can't miss the summer season."

Gia's pulse quickened. That would give her plenty of time to do it if she had the right team. Which Nina assured her she would.

Excitement began to build. Chloe had mentioned a friend who had an excellent nanny who would soon be looking for work. If she could arrange the same sort of schedule she'd had in Nassau this could work. She would feel less like the disenfranchised version of herself she'd been these last few weeks, she could have her career back and still be there for Leo.

Nina handed over her card. They agreed to meet for lunch when the hotelier returned to town the following week, said their goodbyes, then Gia tucked her purse under her arm and headed off to meet Santo, her steps as light as air.

Maybe everything was going to come together in this new life of hers. Maybe it was going to be everything she'd never thought it could be.

They ended up dropping off Lazzero and Chiara on the way home, the two Di Fiore men immersed in a heated discussion about a number for Carl O'Brien in the car. Her exciting news percolating in her head, Gia had to wait until they were back at the penthouse before she could tell Santo. Alone in the private confines of their plush, luxurious dressing-room space, the tension that had been building all night between them swirled against an impressive backdrop of Manhattan.

Santo's fingers paused on the knot of his tie. "Why don't you come over here?" he murmured. "You're much too far away."

His eyes an intense, unfathomable black, she felt the look all the way to her toes. "I haven't told you my good news yet," she murmured, dangling a shoe from her finger. "I bumped into Nina Ferrone on the way out tonight. She needs someone to freshen up the decor at The Billiards Room on the Upper East Side. She wants me to do it."

Santo froze in midmovement. "When?"

"Next month," she said happily. "She's willing to be flexible with my work hours, too. The only caveat is that the job needs to be done by the spring, which shouldn't be a problem at all given the team I'd have."

He stripped off his tie and tossed it on a chair. "Why mess with a good thing?" he said casually. "Leo is doing great. Everything is good between us."

Something about the careful tone of his voice made her pause. "Because I love what I do," she said evenly. "Because this is the perfect opportunity to get my name out there. To have an influential client like Nina to get things jumpstarted for me in New York. It's an amazing opportunity."

"You don't need to get your name out there." He crossed his arms over his chest and leaned back against the dresser. "My wife doesn't need to work, Gia. Leo is just getting settled. He doesn't need any more changes to his routine right now. He needs all of you."

Heat singed her veins. She wasn't sure which inflamed her more. That he was questioning her priorities after she'd spent the last three years putting Leo first, or that he was sweeping her career under the rug, as if it was the insignificant entity it clearly was to him. Exactly as Franco had done.

She came crashing down from her high with a resounding thump. Tossed the shoe on the floor. "I am aware of that," she said tersely. "Leo's welfare has always been my priority, Santo, and always will be. Working and caring for him, however, are not mutually exclusive. I don't *need* to work. I *want* to work."

"So find yourself some smaller projects," he suggested calmly. "Go nuts with the house in Southampton. My boathouse in Maine needs an update. So does my office. Both are sorely overdue."

"I see," she said, bringing her back teeth together. "And when I'm done with that, perhaps I can start on your new walk-in closet? Figure out a better arrangement for those flashy suits of yours? Devise a more economical space solution for your expensive shoes?"

He shot her a warning look. "Gia—"

She reached down and undid the strap of her other shoe, fingers shaking with anger. She slid it off, picked up both shoes, stalked past him to the elegantly appointed footwear closet and tossed the sandals onto a shelf, missing with her aim, the shoes tumbling to the floor.

Santo shot out an arm and barred her exit, a set look on his face. "What is your problem?" he murmured, in a voice too deadly to be soft. "I am giving everything here, Gia. The new house, this marriage, the *patience* I am exhibiting with you. Is it too much to expect that you could be agreeable on this point?"

"Yes," she stormed, heat flaring her cheeks. "I had a life in Nassau, Santo. A dream. A career. I was *happy*. And now I am back in New York, where I don't want to be, I am married to you, which was also not my decision, and now you are trying to take away the one thing that gives my life meaning."

"I am not asking you to give up your career. I am asking you to take a *breather*. To take a step back from ramping things up until Leo is in school, at least. Then, you can arrange your schedule so that you're home when he's finished at the end of the day."

"It's funny," she observed, the anger fizzling her veins threatening to spill over. "The only one who seems to be compromising here is me.

You and your impressive career trajectory remain untouched."

He gave a shrug of his shoulder. "I am a CEO. I run a multibillion-dollar company. I spend every moment I can with Leo. I'm with him every morning and night. I think this arrangement works perfectly for us."

"I'll bet you do." Her hands clenched into fists at her sides. "This is all suiting you, perfectly, Santo. But not me."

"Then how about you try focusing your attention on *me*?" he murmured. "Maybe that will distract you. Leo is three. He's waited long enough for a sibling. Maybe we should get on that."

Her breath caught in her chest. The heat that had been smoldering between them all evening smoked to life. He was so gorgeous in his beautiful suit and sky-blue shirt that molded to every powerful inch of him, it was almost impossible to keep her head on straight. "You don't distract me," she said, biting out the words. "You *irritate* me with your antiquated, chauvinistic, close-minded opinions, Santo. With your *dishonest*, bull-in-a-china-shop approach."

"I didn't lie to you," he countered. "I was clear

about how I felt about Leo being in any type of care. If anything," he drawled, "it was a sin of omission."

A haze of red enveloped her, her nails digging hard into the soft skin of her palms. "And that night we stood here and I reinforced the fact that I wanted to work? And you said, 'of course,' to me?"

Not a flicker of self-recrimination on his hard-boned face. "I do think it's okay. Just not *now*."

She caught her breath at the hard glint in his eyes. The *deliberation*. He had married her knowing he was never going to let her work. Had done it with calculated precision so that once she was married to him, she would have no choice in the matter. Because who else in the city was going to hire her? Who, other than Nina, had the guts to do it?

He took a step closer. Ran a thumb down her cheek. "Come on, baby. You knew my feelings on this. Don't mess this up when we finally have something good. When I am too damn busy to think."

It was the last comment that did it. That his work was so important it obliterated her need to be happy. The red surging in her head consumed her brain. She took a step back. Picked up the first thing that came to hand, a bright red stiletto, and threw it at him. He caught it with those high-octane reflexes of his before it could make contact with the rock-hard muscle of his chest. But it felt so good, so satisfying, she did it again.

It still wasn't enough. Frustration and fear, *fury* consuming her in a mad red haze, she scooped up another shoe and took aim. And then another, until she had emptied a whole row. One sole shoe remaining, she clutched it with shaking hands. Santo gave her a hard look, a glitter in his dark, beautiful eyes that promised retribution. "One more shoe, Gia," he murmured. "*One. More. Shoe.* And all bets are off. Do it at your own peril."

A combination of fear and excitement clenched her stomach tight. Eyes pinned on his, her chest heaving, she took aim, aware of exactly what line she was crossing if she did it, and doing it, anyway.

He moved fast like a cat, like the superior athlete that he was, catching the shoe midstride before he tossed it aside, strode toward her and scooped her off her feet. Stalking through the dressing room, he walked into the bedroom and deposited her on the huge, king-sized bed. He came down over her, his powerful body caging hers.

"We will find a compromise," he insisted. "But there will be no more drama, Gia. Enough of the Mafia Princess act."

*That* made her want to claw his eyes out. She tried to summon the rational part of her brain that should still be working, but the only word her brain could focus on was the word *compromise*. He was willing to *compromise*.

And then he was tracing an erotic path down the line of her throat with that talented tongue of his, his hot, hard erection nudging against her thigh, and she lost the plot completely.

"You should move now if you don't want this," he warned, giving her ample time to put a stop to the insanity that had been building between them all evening. But she couldn't find the words. She had been imagining this all night. Craving it. *Anticipating it*.

He slid her dress up her thighs with a warm palm. Pushed aside the lace panties she wore and traced the slick flesh of her cleft with the pad of his thumb.

"You want me here?" he murmured.

She didn't want to want him, but she did. *Badly.* She arched her hips against his devastating caress that delved deeper with every stroke. Against the thumb he rotated against the tight nub at the heart of her. *"Yes."*

His breath left him on a harsh exhale. Her fingers found the buckle of his belt, the button of his pants. Freed his thick, rigid length. Lifting her hips, she took him deep in a single, powerful stroke that stole her breath.

Buried deep inside of her, she could feel the hard pulse of him, his erection as silken smooth and powerful as the rest of him. He was so deep, so big inside of her—he filled every part of her.

She sucked in a lungful of air. Attempted to find a foothold in the moment. But then, he set those hot, dark eyes on her and they stared at each other for a long, suspended moment, absorbing the power of what they shared. It was almost unnerving, the intensity of it. And then he started to move. One arm at her back, the other in her hair, it was breathtakingly deliberate, every stroke a languid promise, building with every powerful thrust.

Her gaze was riveted to his face. His beautiful

features imprinted with lust, his eyes so dilated and dark they were almost black, he was as lost to the moment as she was.

He lowered his mouth to hers in a deep, slow kiss. Gia closed her eyes and gave in to the storm. Spurred on by the intense fullness inside of her, his undulating, devastating strokes, his bitten-out command for her to come for him, her orgasm swept through her, all-consuming and uncontrollable.

She shook in his arms. Santo drank her cries of completion. Clamped a hand around her thigh, lifted it around his waist and positioned her for his unfettered penetration, so that she caressed his shaft with every stroke. She met his thrusts with a ragged breath, aftershocks of pleasure exploding through her dazed body and soul.

He made her scream before he was done. Made her fall apart all over again. And this time, he came with her, too.

Gia emerged slowly from the ecstasy of surrender. Spent, shattered, she curled up on the soft, silky comforter and watched as Santo rolled off the bed and stripped off the beautiful suit with swift efficiency.

"That was—"

"Insane," he murmured.

*Yes.* That was the word for it. She sank her teeth into her lip as he shrugged off his shirt. "So, regarding this compromise… I'll have lunch with Nina next week and I'll find out more details about the work. Chloe says she knows an amazing nanny who's about to lose a full-time position, which is *gold* in New York. We can meet her and you can dec—"

Santo held up a hand. "I said *compromise.* Meaning we will find a solution to this problem that fits both of us, Gia. Which is not you working for Nina. That job will be manic. You will be on call all hours of the day. There will be no controlling it. What *I* am envisioning is that you start a small business where you can work from home. Take on small jobs, with the nanny here for Leo while you're working. That way, you can have the best of both worlds."

*The best of both worlds?* Her rosy glow evaporated in the millisecond it took him to crush it dead. She sat up on the bed and yanked her dress down over her hips. "And who is going to take me on?" she rasped. "Who, other than Nina, is going to have any interest in working with Stefano Castiglione's daughter? In *associating* themselves with me?"

"If they judge you by your last name," he countered blithely, "they aren't worth your time. You have talent, Gia. If Nina is willing to break ranks, so will others."

"And you saw how well that worked tonight," she observed, a bitter taste in her mouth. "I was top of my class in design school, Santo. It took my fellow students in the top tier one, maybe two tries to get a work placement. Do you know how many tries it took me?" She arched an eyebrow. "*Ten*. They were all terrified of my father. And that was *before* he ended up on the front of every newspaper in the country."

A stubborn look claimed his face. "Then maybe you should focus on family for the time being. It is impossible for two people in a relationship to have high-powered careers, Gia. It simply doesn't work. The children are always the ones to suffer. I won't have that for Leo."

*He wouldn't have that?* "And what about Nico and Chloe?" she challenged. "How are they making this *untenable* situation work?"

The closed look on his face intensified. "They

are not *us*. That isn't what I want out of my marriage."

"No," she agreed, flattened by his implacability, "you want everything. You want me to fall in line with this grand plan of yours. With your vision of what this perfect marriage of ours should look like. You want me to have faith in *us*. And just when I'm beginning to do so, you go and prove you are no more trustworthy than any other man I've ever met, because you knew, *you knew* how important this was to me and you went ahead and did it anyway."

His ebony gaze went wintry and cold. "I did what I needed to do to secure my son. If there is a lack of trust in this relationship, Gia, that would be all on you. You started this with your inability to do the right thing."

She jerked her head back at that cold, verbal slap in the face, any ideas that he might actually have forgiven her gone up in a wisp of smoke. But that didn't mean she was going to let him run roughshod over her. That she would let him strip her of everything she'd fought so hard to become. That she was going to spend her days in another corrosive, unhappy marriage trying to keep him happy while she died a little inside every day, exactly as she had with Franco.

She scrambled off the bed. Recovered her physical and emotional feet. "I'm not interested in your compromise," she told him, chin held high. "When you decide you are serious about making this marriage work, when you are willing to give as much as you are demanding, when you are willing to show that you *care*, you know where to find me."

Frustration painted itself across his face. "Gia—"

She ignored him. Stalked into the dressing room and snatched up a nightie to sleep in before she abandoned ship for the spare room, everything that had seemed so bright and shiny and full of promise demolished in an unequivocal, emotional wreck.

## CHAPTER EIGHT

Santo exited the meeting he'd been attending with his design team at Supersonic's Central Park West offices, secure in the knowledge that the manufacturing flaw they had uncovered in Elevate had been successfully ironed out without detriment to the shoe's design, and production was back on a smooth schedule.

Which was key, because in just a few weeks, the sneaker would be winging its way across the globe and into stores for its worldwide launch, supported by the massive marketing campaign the company had planned. Elevate would soon become the most talked-about running shoe on the planet and all the critics would be silenced.

His marriage, however, was not on that same upward trajectory. It festered like an open wound that wouldn't heal as he picked up the messages his assistant, Enid, handed him before she left for the day, and continued on into his office. Gone were the intimate family dinners that had come to represent the highlight of his day, replaced by short, curt affairs in which Gia chose to communicate with him only when spoken to directly.

Gone, also, were the long, hot nights, replaced by an ice-cold version of her as chilly as the cherry-flavored Popsicles she served Leo after dinner. She wasn't happy, that was clear. Nor was he. In fact, it was so far from the vision of the marriage he'd wanted for himself, it would have been laughable if it hadn't been so damn disconcerting, because he and Gia were at a stalemate and he could not see a way forward.

Never, in his experience, had he seen a high-powered couple make a family work. Nico and Chloe were managing it, but that was the operative word. *Managing.* Even Nico labeled it the supreme juggling act that it was. Chloe had confessed she wanted to spend more time with Jack and had plans to scale back her focus to make that happen. Which only proved his point. So he'd proposed the optimal solution to Gia, only to have her turn it down flat. Which left them exactly nowhere, because she'd gone ahead and had her lunch with Nina instead.

Lazzero strolled into his office. Surveyed him

with a long look. If he made one more comment about *paradise*, he fumed inwardly, he was going to take off his head. His brother, however, seemed to recognize his perilous mood and leaned a hip against the front of his desk instead.

"Carlos just called. We're being asked to give input on the trade deal. He wants reinforcements."

Santo rubbed a hand over his brow. He was knee-deep in orchestrating a one-hundred-million-dollar marketing campaign for Elevate. He was having lunch with the best soccer player in the world on Wednesday, as the athlete was headlining their advertising campaign. And then there was Saturday's dinner with Gervasio Delgado. That the negotiations around the Mexican trade deal would heat up now, when they'd been lagging for months, was impeccably bad timing. But if Carlos Santino, the president of their Mexican subsidiary, had picked up the phone asking for reinforcements, he clearly needed it.

"When?"

"This week." His brother waved a hand at him. "I'll go. I'm better with the numbers and you have more on your plate than I do. Plus the daddy duties. But that means you have to handle Gervasio by yourself. I won't be back in time."

"Fine." He'd met Gervasio Delgado numerous times. They had good chemistry together. Closing this deal would not be a problem.

"Chiara is going to crucify me," Lazzero said drily. "She will be devastated."

"She'll have plenty of time to meet him when we ink this deal." His wife, however, could be a problem. He needed her onside if she was going to charm Alicia Delgado at this dinner. *If* he could get her to talk to him. Which wasn't at all a guaranteed proposition at the moment.

"When will you leave?"

"Tomorrow morning. I need some time to acclimatize before I have to use my brain."

"Good idea." Santo stood and threw some papers in his briefcase, intent on a cold beer, a wrestle with his son and a resolution with his wife. Preferably in that order.

Gia shouldered her way through the penthouse door, a bag of groceries in one hand, a latte from her favorite bakery in the other. Expecting that Anna would have her son in the bath by now, she was instead greeted by Leo's peals of laughter and a rich deep baritone that accompanied it.

Her heart beat a jagged edge. *Santo was home?* She thought he'd be working late tonight, thus the reason she'd taken up Chloe's nanny on her offer of a few hours respite to get some errands done. But when she walked into the living room, her husband was indeed home, lying on the floor, bench-pressing her son as if he weighed nothing. Leo was waving his arms in the air as if he was a *supahero* coming in for a landing.

*"Mamma,"* her son cried. "Look at me. I'm flying."

"Wow," she murmured. "You are."

Santo set down his son on his chest, all of that bulging muscle under his finely woven shirt doing something crazy to her insides. He was indecently gorgeous even when she hated him. "Maybe *Mamma*," he suggested, setting his gaze on her, "should come over and take a turn. She might like it, too."

Gia gave him a frosty look. She wasn't letting him charm his way out of this one.

Leo moved his gaze from one of them to the other, clearly attempting to decipher the mood. "I think," Santo confessed to his son, "that

*Mamma* might be angry with me. What do you think I should do?"

"Flowers," Leo said confidently. "Pink ones."

She almost smiled at that, a memory of Leo emerging, shoulders deep, from Delilah's peony garden with a fistful of pink flowers in his hand and a wicked smile on his face, filling her head. She had been horrified, while Delilah had been thankfully amused.

But nope, that still wasn't touching the ice that encased her.

Santo rolled into a sitting position. "Good idea," he said to Leo. "I will keep that in mind. Did you know," he told him, "that even *supaheroes* need lots of sleep? *Especially supaheroes*, because that's where they get their power from."

Leo's eyes went round. He ran to Gia and gave her an enthusiastic hug, before Santo swooped him up and took him to bed. A discussion about kryptonite ensued, trailing off as they disappeared up the stairs.

Gia took the groceries into the kitchen, stowed them away, then opened a bottle of Chianti she had acquired from the art wall display. Intent on fine-tuning a couple of the drawings she'd done for the Hamptons house, she curled up in a chair in the living room with her sketch pad and a glass of wine.

Santo came downstairs shortly thereafter, dressed in jeans and a T-shirt. She nodded toward the kitchen, without looking up. "I bought home some antipasto from the deli if you're hungry."

"I had a late lunch. I'll join you for a glass of wine, instead."

"Don't bother." She kept her eyes on the sketch pad. "I'm sure you have work to do."

"We need to talk about this, Gia."

She looked up at him. "What's the point? You don't see me, Santo. You only see what you want to see."

Santo regarded his wife's frigid demeanor. Poured himself a glass of wine from the bottle on the table and sat down beside her, stretching his long legs out in front of him. "Tell me, then. Tell me why it has to be *this job*, *right now*. Why it can't be something more manageable. And yes, I know working with Nina is a great opportunity, but there will be other opportunities."

Her chin took on a stubborn tilt. "Because it's an amazing opportunity. Because I can *do it*.

Nina has promised me a crack team. If I manage it correctly, it won't be a problem."

"And when the construction manager calls you at ten o'clock at night with an emergency?"

"I will handle it. Isn't that how *you* do it?" She arched an eyebrow at him. "Surround yourself with good people to get the job done?"

"Yes, but I also work sixteen-hour days. We can't both do that." He considered her over the rim of his glass. "If you don't want to do work for me, then come join Supersonic's design department part-time. We have a massive retail push on at the moment. They could use the help. You'd be a fantastic addition given the work you've done for Delilah."

The stubborn tilt of her chin intensified. "I can't work for you."

He threw up his hands. "I'm trying here, Gia. I'm offering you the money to front a business of your own. *Alternatives*. You have to give a bit, too."

Her long, dusky lashes swept her cheeks. "You need to understand my past. My history."

He swallowed past the bite of frustration that sank into his skin. "Which is?"

She pushed a lock of her hair behind her ear.

"My mother never had what I have, Santo. She was *powerless*. She wanted more for me. She knew what I was walking into with Franco. So, she struck a deal with my father. That I would be able to go to college before I married him. So that I would have an education, something to fall back on if something happened."

"Like what?" Santo asked.

He watched her battle against those internal rules that would have kept her silent, until she finally broke the extended pause. "My father," she said, "has been to jail twice. Once for masterminding an auto-theft ring when he was in his early twenties. Another time for an illegal gambling operation when I was seven. In those days, he was still climbing the ranks. Paying his dues. The *famiglia* took care of us, but there was no money left for anything extra. No dance lessons for me, no cool sneakers for Tommaso. My mother was, essentially, devastated twice in those early years."

*Cristo.* He hadn't known that part. "That must have been difficult," he murmured. "Did you and Tommaso know what was going on?"

Her mouth twisted. "My mother told us he was running the business in Mexico. Another of the myths my childhood was constructed on. But I think," she recalled, eyes darkening, "that underneath it all, we knew something was wrong. My mother was always upset. *Stressed.* Though she hid it well. She is the strongest person I know."

"Like you are." Santo said quietly, eyeing the woman he had come to learn had a core of steel. "You are a lot like her, Gia."

Her mouth softened, a glimmer of an emotion he couldn't read in those deep green eyes. "Which was why," she continued, "my career is so important to me. I told myself it would be my identity when I married Franco. My safety net. And at first," she allowed, "he was fine with it. He liked the work I did on his hotels. *I* loved it. But after I had Leo, when we tried to have our own child, everything went...*downhill.*"

A fist clamped around his chest. He didn't want to hear this part. Didn't want to think about her with another man. But he also needed to know the truth to truly lay those ghosts to rest.

"It wasn't happening for us," she said. "I was intimidated by him. He was cold. *Unyielding.* It seemed the harder I tried to conceive, the more difficult it got. Franco," she said, eyes on his, "was jealous of you. He punished me by refusing to allow me to work. Said I should focus on a family instead. Took a mistress. Which was almost a relief," she allowed. "He turned even colder, more distant, until our marriage fell apart."

A flash of red moved through his head. It was so far from the vision he'd had of her marriage to the powerful, arrogant Italian she'd married, he couldn't even reconcile the two. Franco Lombardi had been a consummate womanizer who'd had his fill of any woman he'd desired. In his head, Gia had been walking into his arms and out of his, no matter how much she'd dreaded it. But in reality, he conceded, consumed by a wealth of emotion he had no idea how to handle, it had been anything but what he'd envisioned.

"But you stayed," he murmured, "because you had to."

Gia nodded. "I thought about leaving. I almost did twice. Delilah had made it clear she would help me. But every time I got as far as packing, I would think about my father and how angry he would be and I couldn't do it."

The misery, *helplessness* of those darkest days, washed over her like a dark cloud. The fear that this would always be her life. "So I stayed," she said. "Acted the part. I hosted Franco's dinner parties, kept myself out of his business—did everything that I was supposed to do."

"Until he was shot outside of his casino," said Santo. "Providing you with the opportunity to leave."

She nodded. "I called Delilah, she got passports for Leo and I under the name De Luca and she flew us out the night after Franco's funeral."

She remembered the wind whipping through her windbreaker, Leo bundled in her arms. How scared she'd been that Delilah's car wouldn't be where it was supposed to be. But it had been and they'd flown through the night to the private airport they'd flown out of.

"I was," she said huskily, "frozen when I arrived at Delilah's. I couldn't believe what I'd done. I was terrified I'd never get away with it. But Delilah made sure we didn't leave any tracks. And eventually, Leo and I settled in. When I was ready," she mused, heart pulsing at the memory, "Delilah gave me a job. I came into myself. I started to believe my life could be different. That *everything* could be different. I was Gia De Luca, not Gia Castiglione. I had a clean slate. I could be everything I ever wanted to be."

"Until I took it away from you," Santo said quietly. "That identity you'd created for yourself."

She nodded.

He dragged a hand over the back of his neck. "I was angry, Gia. You had taken my son. I had missed three years of his life. I did what I thought I needed to do. And yes," he conceded on a heavy exhale, "it's true. I have this vision of what I want my marriage and life to be, but there's a reason for it."

Gia eyed the stubborn lines of his face. "Because you never had it."

"Yes." He took a sip of his wine. "My mother was never mother-of-the-year material. I think on some level, I always accepted that. She was more interested in sitting on her high-profile charities. Expanding her influence. Spending our father's money. We had nannies when she managed to keep them. But she was there. She kept us clothed and fed. She enforced the rules, which we needed because my father was working all the time. She was a buffer between us and the drinking when that became a problem."

He rested his head against the back of the sofa, his eyes dark. "She walked out on New Year's Day. A week later, the bank arrived to repossess the house. I spent the next week in shock, telling myself that my mother would come back. She always did."

*Except this time, she hadn't.* Gia's heart lurched. "Thank god you had your brothers."

He nodded. "But they were immersed in their own internal battles. I would go home from school every day to that empty, depressing apartment and watch my father drink himself into the ground. Until word spread in the neighborhood of what had happened and Mamma Esposito, my best friend Pietro's mother, Carmela, insisted I come to their house after school.

"It was like culture shock for me," he reminisced, his mouth curving. "Kids and laughter everywhere. A basketball hoop in the front yard that attracted half the neighborhood. I didn't talk at all at first. Too heart-sore to do anything more than go through the motions. Mamma Esposito would put a plate of cookies in front of me and say nothing at all. She was just *there*. And gradually," he allowed, "I unfroze. I started to talk to her." His gaze dropped to the ruby-red wine in his glass. "I think she saved me, to be honest. I'm not sure what would have happened to me if it hadn't been for her."

The thought of him so lost, *helpless*, melted her heart. Melted all the ice around her, because all she could remember was Santo being the strong one. Santo and his dreams. His relentless refusal to accept anything less for himself. Everything that he had taught *her*.

She curled her fingers around his. "I'm so glad you had her," she murmured. "Carmela. She sounds wonderful."

"She was." He swirled the wine around his glass in a contemplative gesture. "I had a lot of guilt. That my brothers and I had been too much of a handful. That, maybe, we had driven my mother away. Carmela said something to me that really resonated with me. That maybe, it wasn't that my mother hadn't cared so much as she hadn't been *built for the job*. It was a concept I could understand."

Which was exactly what he wanted in a wife. Her stomach sank as she absorbed the insight into him. How it explained everything about him. About the vision he'd always had of the family he wanted. About the woman he'd wanted in his life. He wanted a *Carmela*.

"I can't be her, Santo," she said quietly. "Carmela. I saw how unhappy my mother was. I saw what her life did to her. I *know* how it affected me. I need my career. My independence. To stand on my own two feet."

"I get that," he murmured. "I do."

She watched the conflict in his eyes. How much it meant to him. And she knew, in that moment, it had the power to make or break them.

"You are a wonderful mother," he said huskily, curling his fingers tight around hers. "I watch Leo and I marvel at how confident he is. How utterly sure he is of his place in the world. You gave that to him, Gia. If you take this job with Nina, it will never contain itself to those hours. It *will* be madness. Leo will suffer. *We* will suffer."

She dug her teeth into her lip, lost in a sea of indecision. It was a big project, even with the team Nina would give her. There was no denying it. Nina was a perfectionist, just like Delilah. But in Nassau, it had been easy to pull out her laptop and work until midnight after Leo had gone to bed, because it had only been her to consider. Which would not be so easy now.

It seemed an impossible decision. She *knew* how unhappy she'd been with Franco. She knew she couldn't be in another marriage like that. But she didn't want to kill her relationship with Santo, either. Not when she had been the one to break them the first time.

"I can do it," she said huskily. "I promise you, Santo. I can make this work. And the reason that Leo is such a confident little boy is that I have learned to become that myself. What kind of a role model would I be for Leo if I didn't teach him to go after his dreams?"

A fleeting series of emotions shifted across his face. She watched him battle his need to control. To *make* this what he wanted it to be. To command this world he had created. Then he finally relented. "Fine," he murmured. "Take the job if you feel that's what you need to do. I can see how much this means to you." He set his wineglass on the table, then reached for hers. "Meanwhile," he said, sinking his hands into her waist and settling her into his lap so that she straddled his thighs, "I think you should kiss me. I am in severe withdrawal. Withering away from the effects of your icy facade."

"Sex will not change my mind," she told him, every cell in her body springing to life as he set his fingers to one side of her neck and his thumb to the other in a gesture of pure possession. "I need this, Santo."

"I know that. I just want you. *Badly.*"

It was the *badly* that did it, because she had been empty without him. Everything had been empty without him. And she wasn't sure how to fill the holes.

She buried her fingers in his hair and kissed him. Soft, achingly good kisses that unfurled a wounded part inside of her. Sighing her pleasure, she traced her mouth over the hard edge of his jaw.

His hands dealt with the buttons on her blouse, his mouth finding the soft skin beneath. Her skirt went the way of her blouse, hiked up to her waist by his sure hands. The fragile barrier of her panties ripped with a flick of his wrist. And then there was only his smooth, dominant possession that tore a gasp from her throat.

Her forehead resting against his, the last fragments of sunlight shifting across their bodies, she made it last as long as she could. Slow and undulating, they moved together, each lazy circle pushing her further toward the point of no return. Toward giving him her heart again. Until his overwhelming, unrelenting possession sent her over the edge, the tremors spreading outward from her center, rippling through her body like living fire, and they came together in a brilliant explosion of pleasure.

## CHAPTER NINE

THEY DINED WITH the legendary Spanish retailing giant Gervasio Delgado at Charles, the most celebrated French restaurant in New York, located on Park Avenue. Steeped in French culinary history, and run by famed chef Charles Fortier, it was renowned for its refined European cuisine, world-class wine cellar and gracious hospitality.

It was also, Gia conceded, one of the most beautiful restaurants in the city. From its soaring coffered ceiling to its elegant neoclassical architecture illuminated by custom Bernardaud chandeliers, its classic white color palette was a perfect blank canvas for the colorful artwork that adorned the walls. The vivid, vibrant works were those of a famous classical Spanish painter, a favorite of Charles, as well of Gervasio, as it turned out.

Santo, dressed in a navy suit and an ice-blue shirt, with a darker, contrasting navy tie, was as focused as she'd ever seen him. Which she completely understood. If Delgado elected to feature an Elevate shoe in the front window of his massively popular retail chain, Divertido, it would become an overnight fashion trend.

Gervasio, still intensely charismatic in his early sixties, had left school at fifteen, according to Santo, to work as a tailor's assistant, exactly as Nico had done to support his family. He clearly liked the Supersonic story...its Cinderella rise to stardom. But mostly, Gia thought, he loved the big-name athletes the company commanded and their potential to add glitter to his brand.

He was also intrigued by the concept of Elevate. Tonight was all about convincing him that Supersonic was the clear strategic choice to place in his front window.

Santo set about making the Supersonic case. It was jaw-dropping to watch him in action—something she'd never had the opportunity to do. His charisma and enthusiasm were infectious as he coaxed the notoriously introverted Gervasio out of his shell in that way he had that drew people to him like a moth to a flame.

Watching the man he had become—one who

ruled the world around him so effortlessly—she felt helplessly aware that he had been the only one she'd ever had eyes for and always would be.

It was clear by the time they had polished off cocktails and the first bottle of crisp, delicious Pouilly-Fuissé, that it was going well, the conversation passionate and animated. While Santo focused his attention on Gervasio, Gia devoted hers to his elegant, beautiful wife, Alicia. With that flawless, classical, impeccable style that Gia found European women carried so effortlessly, Alicia had a passionate interest in interior design, because it influenced the fashion trends she created for Divertido. She was also remodeling her house in Marbella, which made for a wealth of conversation.

She and Alicia were talking color trends when a flutter at the front entrance caught Gervasio's attention. He blinked. Gave the front door a long look. "Is that Stefano Castiglione who just walked in?"

Gia froze in her chair. Her back was to the door, but everything slipped at the shocked look on Santo's face. *It could not be. Not here. Not tonight.*

She turned around. Followed Gervasio's gaze.

Caught sight of her father's silvery dark hair and tall, elegant posture as he spoke with Charles, who'd materialized from the kitchen to greet him and the elegant blonde he had on his arm. His latest mistress, she assumed numbly.

Her fingers clutched tight to the sides of her chair. She heard Santo murmur some sort of affirmation to Gervasio before her father trailed a glittering path through the crowd with his grey gaze, the customary combination of awe and respect he commanded rippling through the packed restaurant. And perhaps, she conceded, a fission of ice sliding up her spine, a tiny bit of apprehension.

She understood it. He was her father. She had loved him as much as she had hated him. *Feared* him. And therein lay the conflict that had ruled her existence. To adore someone— to revere them as larger than life—but to also know what they were capable of.

While the other girls in school had spoken about their fathers' affairs in the bathrooms, or the fast and loose lifestyle they'd acquired while working on Wall Street, she'd been wondering who her father had eliminated the night before.

Her father laughed at something the blonde

had said, the rich, resonant sound making her breath catch in her chest. The hair stood up on the back of her neck as he flicked a glance her way, as if sensing her study. She saw his eyes widen, the proud set of his head as he cocked it to one side and took her in. And then there was only the buzzing in her ears as he acknowledged the table Charles had provided, then turned and made his way through the diners to where she sat, his beautiful companion at his side.

"Giovanna." His smooth, even tone betrayed not a hint of emotion as he came to a halt in front of them. It was all in his dark, deep-set eyes—fury mixed with a smattering of something she couldn't identify. "Forgive me," he murmured. "I had no idea you would be here tonight. Your mother only just mentioned you were back in New York."

Gia inhaled a deep, steadying breath as she stood to greet him, dimly aware that Santo had done the same. Her fingers reached back to clutch the edge of the chair tight. "I've only been back in New York a little while," she murmured. "It's been a bit of a whirlwind."

"I see." Those two words held a wealth of meaning. Her stomach plunged another inch as her father turned to Santo and extended a hand. "Santo. I had been hoping I would run into you. We have some business on the table."

Santo shook her father's hand. *"Mi dispiace,"* he murmured. "I have been swamped. Unfortunately," he said, "we have signed an exclusive deal with Delilah Rothchild for our hotel-related retail efforts for the next couple of years. It will be our focus for the time being."

Her father's gaze glimmered. "So it is," he drawled, inclining his head. "The offer is there if you reconsider." He drew his beautiful blonde companion forward. She was thirty if she was a day, barely older than Gia herself. Her father's tastes clearly hadn't changed. "Julianne, this is my daughter, Giovanna Castiglione."

*"Di Fiore,"* Santo corrected smoothly.

Her father's expression turned glacial. "Of course. *Scusi.* My mistake. An old habit. Julianne," he continued, "runs the Derringer Art Gallery on the Upper East Side. I am considering purchasing one of her pieces."

*As if.* Gia's chest burned as Santo made the introductions to the Delgados, who were watching it all with a bemused countenance. Gervasio, whom her father was clearly interested in meeting, looked distinctly standoffish through it all.

Tension climbed the back of her throat. She thought she might actually throw up, her stomach was churning so violently. Particularly when a long, painful silence then ensued. Her father finally broke the détente, setting his gaze on Gia. "Julianne was just mentioning she needed to visit the powder room. Perhaps we could speak privately outside for a few moments given we haven't seen each other in some time?"

Santo tensed beside her, ready to object. Gia put a hand on his arm. Sucked in a breath. She needed to defuse this situation. *Now.* She also needed to get this confrontation with her father over with before she jumped out of her skin. She'd imagined it in her head so many times, it was beginning to make her a little crazy.

If she was going to own this new version of herself, this strength she'd so painstakingly achieved, now was the time to do it. She could not let Santo fight this battle for her, no matter how much she wanted him to. She needed to do it by herself.

"I think that's a good idea," she murmured.

She flicked a glance at the table. "My apologies. If you'll excuse me for a few moments."

Santo narrowed his gaze, as if considering trampling all over that idea. But after a long moment he nodded and bent his head to her ear. "Five minutes," he murmured.

Gia led the way outside into the lamp-lit court-yard at the back of the restaurant. It was deserted except for a patron smoking a cigar at the far end of the quadrangle. A sparkling fountain threw up a spray of gold into the lamplight, a series of beautifully cut marble figures running through it. It was a beautiful night, the air fragrant and warm as it wafted over her skin. But it was her father who claimed all of her attention as he leaned his tall, powerful frame against one of the stone columns supporting the restaurant's facade.

His anger had always manifested itself in one of two ways. Like a violent storm, which had often swept through their brick Georgian home like a thunderclap, flattening everything in its wake, only to die out just as quickly. Or the slow, silent type that was building in his eyes now as he took her in. "I'm not even sure where to begin," he murmured. "The fact that you walked away without a word, or that you showed up here married to Santo Di Fiore without even the courtesy of a warning."

Gia slicked her tongue along desperately dry lips. She had the feeling he was more caught up with Santo throwing his proposal in his face than he was with her return. Which was her father in a nutshell. She pushed her shoulders back and met the grey fury of his gaze. "I needed some time to find my feet. And you knew why I left, *Papà*. You *knew* I was frightened after what happened to Franco. I didn't feel safe. Leo was not safe. I explained all of it in my note."

*"Your note?"* Her father exploded. *"Your note*, Giovanna? You think it was acceptable to leave a note for your family before you walked out of our lives and disappeared? You thought that a *note* would prevent your mother's broken heart. *Cristo*." He waved a hand at her. "Were you thinking of nothing but yourself?"

Two years of fury and heartbreak caught fire. She drew herself up to her full height and met him head-on. "I was thinking of anything *but* myself when I married a man I didn't love. When I gave up the dreams I had for my life. My *future*. I *did* my duty. I have done it my whole life. And then, I watched as my husband was assassinated by some henchmen in front of his casino." She shook her head. "What if it had been Leo? What if a stray bullet had taken him instead?"

Her father waved a hand at her. "That would never have happened. You were protected."

"Like my husband was?" The fear she'd felt for herself, for her son, curled her stomach tight. "You were at war with the Bianchis. It was never going to end."

"It did end." Her father's mouth flattened. "Don't talk about things you can't hope to understand, Gia."

"At what cost?" She wrapped her arms around herself and hugged them tight. "*At what cost, Papà?* I would do the same thing a hundred times over if I had to. Leo will never grow up in that world. He will never take Franco's place. I have seen what it has done to Tommaso. It will never happen."

Her father considered her for an extended beat, his grey gaze calculating. "Where were you? Before you came back?"

Her spine stiffened. "You don't need to know

that." She would never, *ever* put Delilah or her mother in the crosshairs of her father's wrath.

"You could not have been with Santo," he concluded. "His inability to remain faithful to a woman has been well documented. Which means you were with someone else."

She glued her mouth shut. "And Leo?" he prompted. "Where is he? Clearly the Lombardis will be interested in his whereabouts given they are missing a grandson. It is a critical partnership for me, Gia, in case you have forgotten that particularly pertinent fact."

She cringed, the contents of her stomach roiling as if they might actually make an appearance. The truth had to come out. She knew it. But getting the words out of her mouth seemed impossible.

"Leo is not Franco's son," she finally blurted out. "He is Santo's."

Santo sat at the table as the minutes clicked by and attempted to concentrate on what Gervasio was saying, but failed miserably. His attention was focused instead on the path his wife had taken through the busy restaurant to the courtyard. On what was happening outside. Gia had looked frozen at her father's appearance. Stefano livid beneath that smooth veneer of his. He didn't want him anywhere near his ultravulnerable wife.

Nor had the buzz in the restaurant subsided. The most wanted organized-crime figure in the world was in the building. He'd apparently elected to testify in front of congress next week, and Charles Fortier's elegant establishment was a perfect foil for Stefano Castiglione's gilded image. His image restoration project. It was sending shock waves through the room.

Gervasio said something that flew right over his head. He set down his wineglass. "My apologies," he murmured. "I am distracted. Would you excuse me for a moment? I should go check on my wife."

*"Por supuesto."* The Spaniard nodded. "I would do the same."

He threw his napkin on the table and stood. "Please," he said, sweeping a hand toward the table as their main courses arrived, *"Adelante, por favor.* Enjoy."

He followed the path Gia and her father had taken through the restaurant to the courtyard. Emerged into the warm, sultry night to find them standing under the portico talking in low voices. Gia's voice, at least, was low. The bite in Stefano Castiglione's tone sliced through his skin like a knife as he listened to the exchange. Listened to his wife tell her father the truth about Leo.

*Maledizione*. Why couldn't she have waited for him to do it?

A slow burn slashed her father's aristocratic cheekbones in the lamplight. "Clearly none of the morals you were taught were in play that night when you chose to disrespect not only your husband, but me. When you acted like nothing but a common *slut*."

A haze of red flared through his head. Gia, however, looked undaunted, squaring her shoulders. "And what about you, *Papà*? You disrespect *Mamma* every time you appear with your *mistress* in public. When you humiliate her and treat her as if she is a second-class citizen."

"You cannot compare the two," her father dismissed. "What you did was unforgivable, Giovanna."

"That's enough." Santo enunciated the words quietly as he moved to Gia's side and slid an arm around her. She was shaking like a leaf.

Stefano shot him a lethal look. "I was having a private conversation with my daughter."

"Which is over." Santo met the other man's wintry gaze. "Given you now know the truth, I will tell you how this is going to work."

Stefano arched an eyebrow. "How *what* is going to work?"

"Your relationship with your daughter. Gia has chosen to walk away from her family. She is no longer a Castiglione. You need to respect her wishes."

"Or what?"

"Or this becomes a public battle you want to avoid."

Gia blanched. It was the one thing her father couldn't abide. Negative publicity. It drew unwanted attention to his business practices. Shined a light on the family where it preferred to operate in the shadows. Drew attention to his leadership. Something he had more than enough of at the moment.

Stefano considered Santo with a calculating look. "You are stung because I declared her not good enough for you," he murmured. "Now you want revenge."

"Revenge has nothing to do with it," Santo

said evenly. "You put those shadows in her eyes. It ends now."

A long moment passed, thick and pulsing with tension. It finally ended when Stefano lifted a broad, elegant shoulder. "Have her then," he said, flicking a cold look at Gia. "She is no longer my daughter after what she's done."

He turned and strode inside, leaving a stark silence behind him. Santo surveyed his wife's white, stricken face. She looked shaken, *disassembled*. And why wouldn't she? Her father had just disowned her. Struck her from his life as easily as he did one of his high-priced business deals. He didn't have to wonder how it felt. He knew how it felt, as his mother's parting words echoed in his head even now.

*It's too much, Leone. Three boys and now this. I can't do it. I didn't sign up for this.* As if they had been the dead weight, the *complication* she clearly didn't need.

He absorbed the shock reverberating in Gia's emerald eyes. Smoothed a thumb over her cheek. "Are you okay?"

"It isn't anything I didn't expect," she said huskily. "I knew he would react like that. His honor dictated it. I threw that in his face."

"That doesn't negate how it must make you feel," he said quietly. "Nothing gives him the right to do what he just did, Gia," he said quietly. *"Nothing."*

She blinked as if she was having trouble comprehending it all. Rubbed a palm against her temple. "You shouldn't have taken him on like that. It wasn't wise."

"He needed to know that you and Leo are no longer a part of the Castiglione family," he said grimly. "Now he does."

She inhaled a deep breath. "We should go back inside. The Delgados will be wondering where we are."

Could he ask her to sit through a meal with her father on the other side of the room after what had just happened? After he had taken his wife apart?

Gia read his hesitation. "I'm fine," she insisted, lifting a trembling hand to smooth her hair. "I will not let him ruin this, Santo."

She didn't look fine. But what choice did he have? He could not walk out on this dinner with the Delgados.

He tightened his arm around her waist. "Are you sure?"

"Yes."

Something inside of him shifted at the look of fierce determination in her eyes. He threaded his fingers through hers and led her back into the restaurant. Felt a dozen sets of eyes on them as they walked back to the table. Stefano and his companion were seated at a table near the window. Gia took them in, then resolutely shifted her gaze away.

Gervasio, quiet and circumspect, surveyed them both as they returned. *"Está todo bien?" Everything all right?*

Santo nodded. *"Mil disculpas." A thousand apologies.* "I hope you both enjoyed your meals."

The Delgados ensured him they had. Santo ordered another bottle of wine as he attempted to repair an evening gone awry. But the sight of his wife literally melting into her seat beside him, refusing to show how much she hurt, tore a hole in his insides.

And then, there was also the subtle temperature change at the table. Barely perceptible, but it was there. Gervasio was cooler and more distant than before. Back to his elusive self.

The gauntlet they had to maneuver on the way out was the final exclamation mark on an evening that had descended into a disaster. Spilling onto the sidewalk near the valet stand where the restaurant security held them at bay was a contingent of press, cameras at the ready to snap a shot of Stefano and his companion leaving the restaurant. Completing the debacle of a night.

It wasn't until they were home in the quiet, muted confines of the penthouse that Gia was able to breathe again. Numb, frozen with the protective coating she had formed around herself, she kicked off her shoes, walked to the bank of floor-to-ceiling windows and stood looking out at the lights of the city.

Santo appeared by her side, a glass of amber-colored liquid in his hand. She shook it off when he handed it to her, sure she did not need to feel any more numb than she already did. He pressed it into her hands. "Drink it. You need it. You're as white as a ghost."

She wrapped her fingers around the tumbler and took a reluctant sip. Felt the liquor penetrate her bloodstream, the color slowly returning to her cheeks. But as the shock receded, the nightmare the evening had been illuminated itself in crystal-clear clarity. Her father showing up with his mistress. The scene he had caused. How she had dismantled Santo's evening with Gervasio.

A burning sensation crawled from her stomach into her throat. She might have been out of it, but she could not have missed the way Gervasio had withdrawn after her father had shown up. The way the conversation at the table had never quite recovered. The taken-aback look on the Spanish retail scion's face at the media frenzy outside.

The fist clenching her chest tightened. The newspapers would be plastered with the coverage of her father's testimony. It was going to be a circus. Her mother would be completely unwound. And, she acknowledged, fingers of ice crawling up her spine, her father was going to have a target on his back, because the list of people he could incriminate, take down with him, was a virtual who's who of the criminal underworld. Of Washington. Hollywood.

No one would be safe.

He might elect to plead the Fifth. But would anyone wait to hear him say it? She was afraid they would attempt to eliminate him first.

She turned to Santo, the grim lines etched into the sides of his eyes and mouth making it clear he had already considered those possibilities. "I'm so sorry," she whispered, "about tonight. I've ruined everything. This was exactly what I was trying to avoid."

He shook his head. "It wasn't your fault. It was unfortunate timing. I will smooth things over with Gervasio in the morning."

She leaned against the window frame, jagged glass lining her throat. Blinked back the hot tears that stung her eyes. She would not cry over him. She had known from the day she'd walked away from her family that her father would never forgive her for what she'd done. It was an eventuality she had long accepted. So why did she feel as if she'd been gutted from end to end?

"I don't understand," she breathed, throwing a hand up into the air, "why I even care that he is disappointed in me. Why he still has this power over me when I know what he is. What he is *capable* of. When I came to terms with that a long time ago."

"Because he is your father," Santo said quietly.

"Because you can't separate the two. Because you want him to love you."

Which was true. She'd always wanted her father's love. Always craved it. Even when she'd known better. Even when she'd known she was never going to have it. Even when she knew he wasn't *worthy* of it.

Santo brushed his knuckles across her cheek. "You are better off without him," he said huskily. "He is a sociopath, Gia. Sometimes, you need to let go of the expectations. Stop hoping he will love you and start believing that you are better than that."

The dark glitter of emotion in his eyes caught at her heart. She knew he was talking about his mother. That he learned that lesson the hard way. She also knew he was right. Knew that accepting the facts when it came to her father was a reality that was long past due. But coming to terms with that was another matter entirely.

A tear slid down her cheek. Pooled at the corner of her mouth. Santo closed the distance between them, removed the glass from her hands and gathered her into his arms. "He isn't worth your tears. He never was. You are worth so much more than that."

The tears fell harder, dampening her cheeks and soaking his shirt. He picked her up, sat down on the sofa and cradled her against his chest. Put his mouth to the hot, wet tears and kissed each one away. When she was done, he carried her to bed and held her until she slept, too emotionally depleted, too ragged and ripped apart inside to do anything more.

Unable to sleep, his head spinning from the events of the evening, Santo left a sleeping Gia, pulled on jeans and a T-shirt and went downstairs to his office to work.

He should call Lazzero, who was three hours behind him on west coast time, and give him an update on dinner. But what, exactly, would he say? That Stefano Castiglione had walked into Charles tonight and blown the whole evening to bits? That instead of tying up the deal with Gervasio, he had walked away with the distinct impression the Spaniard was backing off all over the place? That he'd been more concerned about his wife than he'd been about nailing down the most important retailer in the world?

A knot tied itself down low. He had promised himself he wouldn't get emotionally involved with his wife. But he was starting to realize that was an impossibility with Gia. That his instinct to protect her, to care for her, had always been his weak spot. His Achilles' heel. Which was going to be his downfall if he didn't watch it.

The phone call, he determined, could wait until the morning. He would call Gervasio first thing and smooth things over. Make sure he understood the ties between he and Stefano Castiglione were personal and not business.

But Gervasio was on a plane to Madrid the next morning when he tried to reach him, which meant that conversation would have to wait. Lazzero called at 8:00 a.m. while Santo stood with a cup of coffee in his hand, surveying the city as it came to life.

"Please tell me there is some way you were not sitting in Charles when Stefano Castiglione walked in last night."

Santo flicked his gaze over the morning papers, which were strewn across his desk. A photo of Stefano Castiglione and his mistress exiting the restaurant was emblazoned across the front of them. "You are fast off the mark."

"It's all over the internet, Santo. It's impossible to miss."

"We were there," Santo said carefully. "Stefano came over to introduce himself to Gervasio." *As well as to annihilate his wife.* Perhaps not in that order.

Lazzero exhaled a deep breath. "How was Gervasio?"

*Tense. Standoffish.* "I think," he began, "Gervasio is not a fan of Stefano's. But," he assured his brother, "the dinner was good. He loved the ideas we have for the launch. He is clearly hot on the athletes we have. There's a great deal of synergy between the two brands."

"So how did you leave it?" A suspicious note infiltrated his brother's voice. "You closed this thing, right?"

Santo winced. "Not yet."

"What do you mean, *not yet*?"

He gave up any attempts at delicacy. "The temperature was a bit off at the end of the night. Gervasio had his poker face on. I'm not sure what he was thinking."

Lazzero uttered a filthy word. "It doesn't take a rocket scientist to figure it out, Santo. He's the most conservative CEO on the face of the goddamn planet—reputation is everything to him.

Your wife is the daughter of the most notorious organized-crime figure in America. What do you *think* he's thinking? He wants nothing to do with this."

"He didn't say that." Santo's gut coiled. "That is pure projection. He was cagey from the very beginning. I'm not sure I would have gotten a yes out of him last night either way. He needs time to think about it."

There was silence on the other end of the phone. Santo knew what was coming and he headed it off at the pass. *"Do not say it,"* he murmured. "I will fix this, Laz. I will make it happen. But do not go there."

His brother took a sip of his coffee, clearly restraining himself, before he moved on with a curt directive to keep him updated. After a brief status report on the Mexican negotiations, which had bled into the weekend, his brother went off to join the next round.

Tossing his phone on the desk, Santo paced to the window, watching as the sun climbed high into the sky. He would smooth things out with Gervasio. This was business, after all, and if the Spaniard was anything, he was a shrewd businessman. But the longer he stood there, the more he saw the potential for disaster.

He needed to retrieve this and fast. Strike before the damage became too catastrophic.

# CHAPTER TEN

GIA WOKE BY herself in the big, four-poster bed, light pouring through the skylight and spilling onto the silk-covered sheets. The warm glow of another spectacular New York summer day evaporated almost immediately as the aftermath of the night before swept over her like a dark, ominous cloud. Her father walking into the restaurant and destroying everything in his wake. Him declaring her dead to him. Santo holding her until she'd cried herself to sleep.

Her father would cut her off completely. Which would mean he would forbid her mother to see her. A deep ache unfurled inside of her, one that had been a constant companion over the past two years. But it wasn't a prospect she had the capacity to even consider at the moment alongside her more imminent fear that her father might have done irreparable damage to the business relationship between her husband and Gervasio Delgado.

A sense of dread snaking through her, she threw on a T-shirt and shorts and went downstairs to the smell of freshly brewed coffee. Leo, who'd taken to getting up with his father on the weekends, was reenacting a *supahero* battle in the living room, while Santo paced the terrace, talking on his cell phone. He looked, she noticed from his rumpled appearance, as if he'd hardly slept.

She gave her son a big hug, then poured herself a cup of coffee and went in search of the morning papers. They were strewn across Santo's desk. The curl of dread inside her intensified as she flicked through them, scanning the headlines. Castiglione to Testify... But Will He Tell All? said one. Crime Boss Turns Himself in Amid Much Fanfare, said another. And from the most respected Washington daily: Castiglione to Take on the Capital in the Best Show in Town.

*Oh, my god.* Almost all of them included a photo of her father and his mistress, Julianne Montagne, leaving Charles in a hail of flashbulbs. Gia's stomach bottomed out at the glossy pictures. It would kill her mother.

She picked up the Washington paper. Scanned the story. Her father had indeed returned to the country to testify, confirmed his lawyers. But he had not given any indication as to whether he would comply with the attorney general's "witch hunt," or whether he would invoke his right to protect himself against self-incrimination, which she felt sure he would do.

Clearly, the attorney general had anticipated the same. According to the article, the brash new figure at the helm of the American justice system was considering prosecuting anyone who failed to participate in a "full and open manner." Which, the journalist opined, was undoubtedly directed toward Stefano Castiglione, the biggest and brightest star on his agenda. Which put her father in an impossible position. Betray his underworld contacts or risk being thrown in jail.

"You're up." Santo strode toward her, phone in hand, all loose, long-limbed elegance in jeans, a T-shirt and bare feet. Hair ruffled, dark eyes piercing, he looked so gorgeous, so warm, so solid, she wanted to throw herself in his arms and have him make it all better. But the distracted look on his face kept her where she was, the kiss he brushed across the top of her head disappointingly brief. "Don't read that," he murmured. "It is nothing but speculation."

She rested back against his desk. "He will have a target on his back."

"Which he is well aware of," Santo said evenly. "None of this is yours to take on, Gia. You are a Di Fiore now. You are no longer a Castiglione. Let your father fight his own battles."

"I'm not worried about him," she said quietly. "I am worried about my mother."

"She is surrounded by family. She'll be fine."

She knew that was true, but she wanted to see it for herself.

He read the thoughts running through her head. "You aren't going anywhere near Las Vegas, Gia. We agreed on this. Your mother decided it was for the best. It is far too politically explosive."

Because of the Lombardis. She wrapped her arms around herself, knowing he was right. Hating how helpless she felt. "Did you get a hold of Gervasio?"

"No." A grim, one-word answer. "He's on a flight back to Madrid. I'll try him later."

She nodded. If she'd had any hopes she'd overblown the damage her father had done to Santo, they vaporized now with the look on his face. He was in problem-solving mode. He needed to fix this. And given the brewing media storm, it was only going to get worse.

"I'm sorry." She didn't know what else to say, except say it again.

"It's not your fault." He dismissed it with a wave of his hand. "Go take Leo for a walk. Get it out of your head. Concentrate on the life you have now. The family you have around you. All of the opportunities in front of you, rather than the circus show your father is putting on. That part of your life is over."

She inclined her head. Looked for some sign of softening in him, some tiny piece of the re-assurance she craved, but he looked utterly pre-occupied.

If the wounded, ragged edges inside of her found this cooler, more distant version of him disconcerting after how tenderly he'd held her the night before, she pushed it aside. All she could hope was that Gervasio signed that deal.

She did her best to do exactly what Santo had said and put that piece of her life behind her over the next couple of weeks, rather than focus on the sensational media coverage of her father's pending testimony in Washington. Taking the job with Nina, putting her world firmly beneath her feet, was exactly how to do it.

If she thought Nina might back out of their agreement once the worst of the scandal hit, the worldly, hard-edged real estate tycoon surprised her, and merely lifted an eyebrow when Gia brought up the topic at lunch.

"Darling, if you've seen as many political storms as I have, you'll know this, too, shall pass," the woman insisted. "Put your head down and get the job done. And hold it high when you walk out of this room. If everyone in this city were defined by their pasts, we'd all be dead on arrival. It's what you do with it that counts."

Buoyed by Nina's firm backing and her sage advice, so like Delilah's, Gia buried herself in her work, excitement sizzling in her veins at the return of her creative outlet. Which was a welcome distraction, given how absent her husband had been in the lead-up to the Elevate launch.

He came home in time for dinner per the routine they'd established, but as soon as it ended, he went off to his office to work until the early hours, after which he came to bed and didn't wake her. She told herself he was swamped, buried under a mountain of work, but she couldn't shake the feeling that something was wrong. That he had withdrawn since that dinner with Gervasio. That it had torn something between them, that fragile bond they had been building. The situation wasn't helped by the complete lack of physical intimacy between them—the one part of their relationship that had always given her confidence in them.

It threw her. Unnerved her. Hurt her. Unearthed all her vulnerable points. Because this was exactly how it had started with Franco. He had wanted her, desired her in the beginning, but when it had become clear that she was less than the asset he'd signed on for, he'd grown cold.

Maybe, she acknowledged as she walked home from the hotel on another gorgeous, sunny day, she was overreacting. Maybe, she determined, pushing all of the negative thoughts out of her head, all they needed was a chance to reconnect. A nice dinner tonight before he left for Munich. Something to reassure herself that everything was fine.

An action plan in place, she picked up the groceries to make Santo's favorite dish, as well as an excellent bottle of wine to go with it, then went home to relieve Leo's new nanny for the day. Tia was Dutch, in her midtwenties and completely adorable. She reminded Gia of Desaray, with her energetic, enthusiastic manner, and Leo loved her. Which had been a huge relief, because Santo liked her, too.

She checked in with her husband, who said he'd be home a bit later tonight, after eight, he thought. Which fit perfectly with her plan. She'd put Leo to bed and have dinner waiting for him when he came home. They would have a romantic night together and she could put all these crazy doubts to rest.

She prepared the intricate beef dish she was making, put it all together and left it in the fridge before she went for a swim with Leo. They played together in the hot afternoon sun, enjoying the perfect weather, before she bathed him, fed him and put him to bed.

Dinner in the oven, she showered and put on the dress she knew Santo liked the best. The one he couldn't resist. A body-skimming, knee-length, wrap design in a sky-blue, it made the most of her curves.

She set a candlelit table on the terrace and turned on some music, a sexy, Spanish guitar CD that fit her mood. Then she curled up in a chair in the living room with a glass of the wine and waited for Santo, her heart thudding with anticipation.

Eight o'clock came and went. Eight thirty. Nine. He finally walked in the door at nine fifteen, as night fell over the city. Dropping his briefcase on the floor of the marble entryway, he walked into the living room and threw his jacket over the back of a chair.

His gaze flicked to the candlelit table on the terrace. To the open bottle of wine. A frown knit his eyebrows together. "*Mi dispiace.* I didn't know you were cooking a special meal."

"It was a surprise." She uncurled her legs from beneath her and stood up. "I thought we could spend some time together before you left."

An apologetic look slid across his face. "I have a report I need to review for a meeting tomorrow and a contract to get back to my lawyer tonight."

Her heart slid to the floor. And so, he couldn't spend even half an hour with her? A man who ran a multibillion-dollar company, as he was so quick to point out to her? A man who likely had his whole legal team on a 24/7 retainer?

A slow burn lit her cheeks. "That's fine," she

murmured. "It's probably burned anyway. It's been in there since eight."

He flicked a glance at his watch. "I could probably spare a few minutes."

"Don't bother," she said curtly. "Get your work done."

"Gia—"

She shook his arm off and stalked into the kitchen, where she dumped the entire contents of the casserole dish into the garbage with no appetite to eat it herself.

Upstairs, she stripped off the beautiful blue dress and tossed it on a chair, her skin stinging. She hadn't been imagining the distance he'd put between them—it was a very real thing she'd been willfully avoiding.

A buzzing sound filled her ears. Spread through her body, sensitizing her skin until it hurt to touch. *It was happening all over again.* What always happened when she allowed herself to believe a relationship could work. That who she was wouldn't eventually destroy it. She always proved herself wrong.

She went through her bedtime routine in robotic fashion, consumed by her thoughts. She'd built up this hope inside of her that she and

Santo could someday have what they'd once had. Something even more powerful and stronger with who they'd become. That someday, it might even grow into love. But he was never going to let himself feel the way about her that he once had. That he was always going to hold a part of himself back. Offer her the slim pickings of the emotional connection he'd put on the table. That he'd now, apparently, decided to rescind.

She curled up in bed, miserable and numb. She'd done exactly what Santo had asked of her. Put herself out there. Met him halfway. Sought that intimacy between them he'd demanded. And look where it had gotten her.

She woke for work after a terrible sleep, dark circles ringing her eyes. Santo had left in the early hours. He'd propped a handwritten note by the coffee machine that she was to take Deacon, his personal bodyguard, to work with her while he was in Germany and leave Benecio with Leo and Tia.

Nothing more. No added message.

Her stomach curled into another knot in a sea of them. She didn't think it was necessary, but she kept her mouth shut and took the big hulk of a man to work with her to keep her husband happy.

It was an exciting, busy day. But the more it stretched on, the more the confrontation played on her mind. Ate away at her insides. It made her feel even more lost in the storm than she already was. Her life had been blown wide open, and now the one person she had thought she could depend on wasn't there for her. The one person she needed desperately.

Her husband called only once, a short, stilted conversation when he'd been on the way out to a dinner. It made the apprehension inside her grow into a disconcerting force, because he couldn't have sounded more distant, more wrapped up in his busy trip.

By the time the week ended, she was exhausted. She put Leo to bed, poured herself a glass of wine and walked out onto the terrace as a resplendent pink sunset lit Manhattan in a golden glow. She could have accepted Chiara's offer to drop by with a bottle of wine, but she hadn't been able to face it. To try and pretend to the vibrant, happy, madly-in-love Chiara that everything was okay when nothing was. When Santo hadn't touched her in weeks. When she was in love with her husband and she was afraid he was never going to let himself love her back. When it felt as if her marriage was slipping away from her and there was nothing she could do about it.

She stood there for a long time, until finally, she picked up her cell phone and called her husband in Munich. It rang a dozen times before he picked it up. He was laughing, a husky sound of amusement in his voice, as he clipped out his customary greeting. "Di Fiore here."

Gia stilled, caught completely off guard by the sexy laughter in his voice. By the sound of loud music pulsing in the background. He was at a party, she realized. *Relaxed.* Nothing like the version of him she'd encountered over the past couple of weeks.

She swallowed past the tightly constricted muscles of her throat. "It's Gia."

"Gia?" he answered, a frown in his voice. "Is everything okay?"

"Yes… I—" Her voice trailed off. What exactly was it that she'd wanted to say? She didn't even know.

"Gia." The frown in his voice deepened. "What's up? Why are you calling?"

*Because she'd wanted to hear his voice. And wasn't that silly?*

"Santo," a musical female voice sang out, close enough to the phone that she was undoubtedly hanging off his arm in that ritualistic exhibition she'd seen so many times. "I have someone you need to meet. We're opening a bottle of champagne at the bar."

Gia's stomach plunged. She knew that voice. That sultry, lazy drawl could only belong to one woman. She'd spent enough time that night at the Met gala obsessing over it. The fact that Santo was with Abigail Wright at an after-hours party that could hardly be all business caused her chest to tighten. The fact that she was introducing him to someone as if it was her rightful place to be at his side drove a stake right through her heart.

*His inability to remain faithful to a woman has been well documented.* Her father's cutting appraisal of her husband flashed through her head. The dozens upon dozens of women he had gone through in the past few years. Franco's extracurricular affairs that had cut a swath of humiliation through her.

"Gia?" Santo's voice deepened as he seemed

to move farther away from the music. "Talk to me. What's going on?"

"Nothing." A bolt of fury moved through her. Here she'd been putting herself through the ringer over him. Agonizing over that confrontation they'd had. Desperate to right this thing between them before it capsized completely. But her husband clearly didn't feel the same. He was out partying with his friends. Cozying up with the woman who should have been his wife.

"I'm fine," she said evenly. "Leo wanted me to send you a kiss. There. Now it's done. You can go."

"Gia—"

She hung up the phone. Tossed it on the table. Stood looking out at the skyline, arms hugged around herself as her mobile vibrated with three more calls, then fell silent.

Let him stew. Let him feel one-tenth of what she was feeling. Her chest felt too sore to breathe. Too hurt to function. She braced her palms on the railing and drew in a deep breath. When had she started to believe this marriage was real? That it could work? That she could ever, even remotely be what Santo wanted or needed? When had she become that much of a fool?

A wet heat stormed the back of her eyes. She blinked it back, furious at herself. She'd thought she could do this. That she could live in another convenient marriage for Leo's sake. But she knew now that she couldn't. That it would break her heart to know that Santo had only married her for Leo. That she would always be his default choice.

That he would make it work, even as he resented her more every day for it. Because she knew he would. She'd been through this. Except this time, it would be worse, because she loved Santo. She always had.

She finally stumbled to bed in the early hours. Rose the next morning to Leo's cheerful explosion of limbs in the big four-poster bed.

*"Mamma,"* he cried, pressing a slobbery kiss to her cheek. It unraveled the tidal wave of emotion that had been inside of her all week, until the tears were a storm sliding down her cheeks.

Leo hugged her, bemused. *"Mamma* okay?"

She nodded. Pressed a kiss to the top of his head through the blinding tears. She cuddled him close until they finally slowed. She was about to get out of bed and get breakfast when her cell phone buzzed on the bedside table. She picked it up and stared at it through bleary eyes, wondering if it would be her husband. She was ridiculously disappointed when it was not. It was a Las Vegas number instead.

She sat up and took the call. The blood drained from her face at the sound of her Aunt Carlotta's voice on the other end of the phone. Short and to the point, her aunt told her that her mother had been admitted to the hospital with chest pains. A *cardiac episode.* How serious it was, they weren't sure.

Gia sank back against the pillows, her heart in her mouth. Her mother had never had any heart problems, but the stress of her father's pending testimony had been awful.

She pushed her disheveled hair out of her eyes. Santo had forbidden her to go to Las Vegas. She would be breaking their deal if she went. But she couldn't not go. It was her mother.

Grim resolve moved through her. To hell with Santo. To hell with her father. To hell with all the men in the world she'd let tell her what to do. She was going.

She took Leo down for breakfast. Benecio was in the kitchen making a coffee. "You okay?" he queried, eyeing her red eyes.

"Actually, I'm not feeling well," she lied. "I think Leo and I will stay in and watch some movies today. If you have things to do, feel free."

He studied her for a moment, then nodded and melted off. Gia, aware that her window of opportunity was short, fed and dressed Leo in record time. Her son eyed her as she carried one of Santo's expensive, high-tech suitcases out of the storage closet and threw it on the bed. Started dumping their clothes into it.

His eyes lit up. "Going on a trip? Take a plane?"

"Yes," she confirmed.

"To see *Papà*?" he asked excitedly.

"No," she said. "To see *Nonna*. Go find Rudolfo," she instructed. "And your blanket."

Leo rounded up his teddy bear and blanket as fast as his little legs would carry him. Gia finished packing while she booked flights on her mobile. In less than an hour she and Leo were wheeling the suitcase out the door.

Her son looked up at her, confused. "Take Benecio?"

"No," she said evenly. "We're giving Benecio the day off."

* * *

Santo stepped into the penthouse at close to noon as a brilliant summer day cloaked New York in bright blue sunshine. His eyes were burning, his brain shot, every muscle in his body making itself known after his whirlwind four-day trip to Europe. But it had been imminently successful.

He'd engineered a meeting with Germany's largest retailer, followed that with a slew of smaller appointments, then closed out the conference with a keynote speech that had brought the audience of thousands of youth to its feet. If that hadn't been enough to make him a dead man walking, he'd tacked on a last-minute side trip to Madrid to talk Gervasio around.

Which he had. *Grazie Dio.*

In the end, it hadn't simply been his business arguments that had won the Spaniard over, but Supersonic's impeccable track record, too. It had overshadowed any doubts the Spanish CEO might have harbored about his personal connections to the Castiglione family. And so, with a request from Gervasio to pass his best along to Gia, they had shaken on the deal and Santo had headed home.

Which, he conceded as he set down his suitcase in the marble foyer, had been an issue he'd put on the back burner for the last couple of weeks. Allowing himself to engage with his beautiful, tempestuous wife, immersing himself in the passionate relationship they shared, sinking any deeper into that emotional realm with her than he already had was exactly what he couldn't do when everything depended on him getting through this next week, this last big push to the Elevate launch, with a clear head.

He had, however, brought with him an olive branch in the bouquet of red roses he held in his hand. He stepped into the living room, where he was greeted by silence. Maybe Gia and Leo had gone out for a walk. Impatient to see his wife and son, he fished in his pocket, found his cell phone and called Benecio.

*"Ciao,"* he greeted him. "Where are you?"

"On my way back to the apartment," his security team member said. "Gia isn't feeling well. She's staying in today."

Santo frowned. "She isn't here."

There was a pause on the other end of the line. "I'll be right there."

Santo tried Gia's cell, but it went to voice mail. Maybe she'd gone to the drugstore for some medication. But why, then, hadn't she let Benecio know? And why wasn't she answering her phone?

He tried her cell again with the same result. Tamped down the frisson of unease that slid through him. She and Leo were undoubtedly fine. But the fact that there were those who would use anything they could as leverage against Stefano Castiglione as he stood poised to testify, including his wife and child, was a reality he couldn't ignore.

He called Gia's cell a third time. This time, she answered. Relief settling through his bones, he frowned at the echo of public announcements in the background. "Where are you?"

"I'm in Las Vegas." Her short, cursory statement had him straightening like an arrow. "My mother has had a heart attack. She's in the hospital. Stable. They think it was a minor one. They're going to run some tests and see how much damage was done."

He raked a hand through his hair. "Thank goodness it was a minor one. Why the hell didn't you call me?"

There was a pregnant silence on the other end of the line. His eyes widened. "Your mother is in the hospital, Gia. What did you think I would do?"

"I thought you'd forbid me to come. I know I'm breaking our deal, Santo, but I need to do this. She is all I have."

"In your family," he corrected in a distracted voice. "You have Leo and I. My family." He buried a hand in his pocket and strode to the window, the skyline spread out before him. "*Cristo.* I have back-to-back meetings in the morning and the launch event on Wednesday. I can't get out there."

"It's fine," she murmured. "I don't need you here."

Something in the way she said it, the dead tone to her voice, raised the hairs on the back of his arms. As if all her walls were back up and she'd built them ten times stronger. "Gia," he said quietly, "I realize things were a little off between us before I left. But it's been crazy, you know that." He glanced at his watch. "I can fly out there for a couple of hours now."

"No." Her voice was flat. Decisive. "I need to do this on my own. I need some time to think."

"About what?" he asked carefully.

"About us. About everything."

*Us? Everything?* It was a big, blinking red caution sign that chilled his blood. "What are you talking about? You can't just throw this at me."

Someone calling his wife's name sounded in the background. "I have to go," she said. "Give me some time, Santo. It's what I need."

The line went dead. He stood staring at the phone, utterly unsure of what to do. He could not believe she had just thrown that at him. Now, when he was utterly unable to do anything about it.

Benecio chose that unfortunate moment to walk in. Santo gave him a savage look. "Which part of 'do not let them out of your sight' did you misinterpret?"

His bodyguard gave a helpless shrug. "She said she was sick. This building is beyond secure. I came back to check on her earlier and the bedroom door was closed. I assumed they were taking a nap."

*Should he have gone in?* his bodyguard's raised eyebrow queried.

Santo blew out a breath. Truthfully, it was not Benecio's fault. Gia was a professional at evading her bodyguards. One helpless look from those big green eyes and she would have had Benecio eating right out of the palm of her hand.

"She's in Vegas," he rasped.

Benecio's eyes widened. "Do you want me to go after her?"

He debated the thought. It would make him feel better to know Gia had his security team with her. But the Castiglione family would be under lockdown right now. It would be an armed fortress. They wouldn't be in any danger. And his wife had made it clear she wanted nothing to do with him.

He shook his head. Dismissed his bodyguard. Made himself an espresso and stood, nursing it in his hands as he considered the day unfolding around him.

He had known he had hurt Gia, blowing off dinner like he had. But it had been all he could do to keep his head straight. To get to the next thing in front of him. To get through the storm he'd been in. He had, however, intended to smooth things over when the madness was done. Which had clearly been a mistake.

His wife might have sounded confused, but he couldn't mistake the message that had come through. It had been loud and clear. She was having second thoughts about them. *Reconsidering them.*

His head flashed back to the words he'd heard from the hallway, his softball glove in his hand, before his mother had walked out.

*I can't do this, Leone. I didn't sign up for this.*

It paralyzed him for a moment, a bolt of pure fury moving through him. Because wasn't this always the way with Gia? She held things inside, bottled them up and refused to address them. Except, he allowed with a sinking realization, she *had* reached out to him. The night she'd cooked dinner for him. When she'd called him in Munich. When she'd sounded so lost on the phone.

He'd been preoccupied, focused on the networking he'd been doing. Had, in his defense, tried to call her back. But she hadn't wanted to hear what he'd had to say. Now his wife was in Las Vegas without his protection, he had no idea where her head was at, and he had a wicked week ahead of him in which he had no time to breathe.

Gia and her Aunt Carlotta took turns at her mother's bedside over the next couple of days as her condition continued to improve. The damage to her mother's heart, according to the doctors, had been limited in nature. Nothing that was irrecoverable with the right medication and the opportunity to heal.

A crush of family came and went, most of it from her mother's side, which was a relief, because the cool response she received from the Castigliones, including her brother, Tommaso, made it clear they would prefer she not be there at all. Her Aunt Carlotta, formidable by anyone's standards, silenced them all, installing she and Leo in her home and ensuring her nephew was surrounded by his cousins, whom Leo bemusedly seemed to accept as yet another facet of his new life.

Her father, she discovered, planned to take the Fifth when he testified later this week, rather than reveal his inner circle. He believed his expensive legal team would prevail. Which, her aunt declared with dismissive disdain, was what had driven her mother into the hospital in the first place, Stefano's *arroganza*. This circus show he was performing.

Finally, Gia got a chance to spend some time alone with her mother. It was disconcerting to see her like this, her mother's olive skin pale beneath its usual warmth, her familiar bergamot scent an elusive whisper against a sterile hospital backdrop, her dark, exotic features, so like her own, strained from the trauma of the past seventy-two hours. To watch her mother's almond-shaped eyes fill with tears at the sight of Leo, whom she hadn't seen since he was six months old.

"He is so much like Santo," her mother murmured. "The spitting image. I think if you had stayed, it would have been difficult to hide it."

Gia's throat tightened at the mention of her husband. At the distance between them it seemed impossible to bridge. Her mother's gaze sharpened. Issuing a request for Carlotta to take Leo off to get a treat, she motioned for the nurse to leave the room. Alone, she wrapped her cool, frail-boned hand around Gia's.

"Tell me what's wrong."

Gia lashes swept down. "Am I that transparent?"

"Only to me." Her mother's mouth softened. "You have been telling me about this beautiful new home you and Santo have bought on the beach. About your fabulous new job. How much Leo loves his new life in New York. Everything seems wonderful, no? So why do you look so sad?"

Tears stung her eyes, a reflexive reaction only her mother could provoke. As if she was five years old again with a scraped knee.

"It's Santo," she confessed. "He's been distant. *Off.* Ever since that dinner with Gervasio Delgado. I'm afraid it's broken something between us and I don't know how to make it right. That it's turning into my marriage with Franco all over again and I don't know what to do about it."

Her mother rested a dark-eyed stare on her. "Santo is not Franco, Gia. Nor is he your father. He is a good man who cares about you. Your marriage is never going to turn into the one that it was." She arched a dark eyebrow at her. "You said he has been busy with this big business thing of his. That he has a great deal of pressure on him right now. Maybe that's all it is."

Maybe it was. She'd told herself that a million times. But she also knew in her gut, that Santo had been different. That he had withdrawn. And the ghosts from her past were too strong to ignore.

Her mother's gaze softened. "Have you talked to Santo? Told him how you feel?"

"I'm afraid to." Her biggest fear uprooted itself and came tumbling out of her mouth. "I'm afraid he's never going to let himself trust me again. That I broke something between us when I walked away with Leo. That I will never be his first choice."

Her mother's brow furrowed. "Why would you think that? He was crazy about you, Gia, that was clear. It was enough that your father stepped in."

"Because of who I am," she said quietly. "Because I'm afraid it will break us over and over again until he won't want to be with me."

Her mother sat back against the pillows, a dark glint in her eyes. She was silent for a long moment before she spoke. "I think you are assuming a great deal of things, *mia cara*. That you will never know the answers to these questions unless you ask him." She shook her head. "You have an opportunity to have everything I never had. A marriage of your own choosing. One that is based on love and affection. And yes," she conceded, "I know Santo pushed you into it, but given that you are in love with him, that once, he was all that you wanted, is it not worth the effort to find out if you are right or if you are wrong?"

Gia swallowed hard, past the lump constricting her throat. It wasn't about the effort. She wasn't sure she could bear to hear the answer. That of all the rejection she'd suffered in her life, Santo was the one person she didn't think she could handle it from. The one who could break *her*.

Her mother squeezed her hand. "You've been running from your feelings for a long time, Giovanna. It's time you stopped and admitted what they are."

She knew her mother was right. In her heart, she knew Santo still had strong feelings for her. It was there in the things he said and did. In the way he'd held her after her father had taken her apart. It was the fact that he might never fully let himself go there that terrified her.

*It might have been complicated, but I thought it was worth it.*

Her heart took a perilous leap. Maybe, it was her turn to take the next step. To tell Santo how she felt. To make everything right she'd wronged four years ago when she'd walked away from him. To jump in with both feet and hope that her gamble that he could love her again wouldn't shatter her.

She had fought for everything else in her life. Maybe it was time she fought for Santo.

# CHAPTER ELEVEN

FLASHBULBS REFLECTED off the step and repeat banner at Liberte, Manhattan's new hot spot in Chelsea, as celebrity after celebrity arrived on a sultry summer night that held the city in a steamy, breathless thrall. The club had its outdoor misters firing, showering the crowd with a cool, refreshing spray, but nothing could quell the guests' enthusiasm for Supersonic's big night.

The invitation-only Elevate party was, officially, the hottest ticket in town. Every fashion, sports and celebrity influencer from around the globe was making their way up onto the dais for their moment in the spotlight. And if the stacked guest list wasn't enough to prove it, the buzz from fashion's inner circles was. The celebrity-backed shoe was about to become the most coveted accessory on the planet, and no one wanted to miss its debut.

From the lit, buzzing entrance, guests descended a flight of stairs into an ethereal oasis. A world of sensory pleasure. The entire space was done in black and white to reflect the sleek, impactful ad campaign, accented by splashes of Supersonic red. Beautiful waitstaff dressed in black circulated with trays of a dark-fruit martini, while projected against the stark white walls were massive video images of the elite athletes who starred in the Elevate ad campaign, accompanied by inspirational messaging of how Elevate had helped raised their game. It was the only nod toward business on a night meant for celebration, other than the sneaker itself, subtly interwoven into the decor on raised, lit displays.

Santo stood at the center of it all, leaning a hip against the gleaming gold bar. To his left stood the president of America's biggest retail chain. To his right, Carl O'Brien, the star quarterback he'd signed today, minus Abigail, who'd decided it wasn't a match made in heaven. In front of him, the highest-paid soccer player in the world partied with his entourage. And somewhere in the crowd was Gervasio Delgado, who had flown in from Madrid for the event.

It should have been the most important night of his life. The culmination of a decade's worth of work spent developing and bringing to market the most important product in his company's history. The night Elevate took the world by storm. Instead, he felt numb. Dead inside. Unable to work up the enthusiasm he should have possessed in what was undoubtedly a triumphant moment, because his wife wasn't there to share it with him. And nothing felt right without her.

Worse, he was beginning to think it was all his fault. That he had been so busy trying to keep it all together, with trying to make this night happen, with keeping his wife at a distance, so afraid strong, spirited Gia would shatter his heart again, he might have destroyed the amazing thing they'd been building.

He tugged at the collar of his silver-grey Armani as an A-list Hollywood actress droned on about her latest effort, his mistakes imprinting themselves in Technicolor detail. He'd made so many of them when it came to Gia, he didn't even know where to start.

He'd forced his wife into a marriage she hadn't wanted. Had excused his bullish behavior by convincing himself he was doing the right thing. By telling himself it was all about his son and his well-being when, in actual fact, what he'd wanted was Gia.

Then, he'd compounded the problem by refusing to admit how he felt. By fooling himself into believing he'd never let himself love his wife again, when he clearly did. By distancing Gia in the moment she'd needed him the most.

Which, he acknowledged, knocking back a sip of bourbon on a bitter wave of self-recrimination, illuminated his true Achilles' heel. That he was so afraid of becoming his father—of repeating those same mistakes he'd made—he hadn't seen what was right in front of him. That in the imperfect family he'd been handed, he had everything he could ever want and more.

The actress wandered off, finally absorbing the fact that he'd heard nothing of what she'd said. Nico and Lazzero materialized by his side, a bottle of vintage champagne and three glasses in his eldest brother's hands.

"For a man about to take over the luxury sneaker market," Lazzero drawled, "you are looking a little less than over the moon."

He shrugged a shoulder. "The adrenaline rush. You have to come down sometime."

An enigmatic smile touched his brother's

mouth. "Not for a while, *fratello*. I just got the first day's sales. They are through the roof."

That made a little dent in the numbness encasing him. But not much. He summoned a modicum of enthusiasm as Nico poured the champagne and proposed a toast. "To Elevate. May it wipe the competition from the face of the planet."

He took a sip of the excellent vintage. Attempted to follow the conversation as Nico made a very male comment about the beautiful dancers he was studiously ignoring on his wife's command, a topic Santo couldn't add to because he'd only glanced at them once to make sure they were doing their job.

Nico gave him a long look. "What the hell is wrong with you? This is your big night."

"Her name starts with a *G* and ends with an *A*," Lazzero supplied drily. "I feel like this is becoming a bad habit," his brother drawled, "but maybe you should just turn around."

Santo spun on his heel to find Gia standing at the entrance to the club, perched at the top of the stairs that led to the crowded space. Clad in a fire-engine-red dress, her hair tucked behind her ear in a sleek, sophisticated style that skimmed her cheeks, her legs endless in the figure-hugging outfit, her dark looks contrasted against the bloodred color, she looked ravishing.

Apparently, he wasn't the only one to notice, because a whole contingent of men had turned to stop and stare. It was her confidence, however, that held Santo riveted. Shoulders squared, head thrown back, she looked utterly sure of herself. *Defiant. Determined.* Not a trace of the hesitancy he was so used to seeing in her.

Something deep in his chest constricted. Filled him with a deep throb that bloomed and grew into something so big and powerful, it was hard to catch his breath. She had weathered the storm of the last couple of weeks with that backbone of steel she'd acquired. Had refused to succumb to it. She was, without a doubt, the strongest, most courageous woman he knew.

In that moment, everything was crystal clear. He'd told himself he'd wanted a cookie-cutter wife. A woman who would fit perfectly into the seamless, even-keeled world he'd constructed for himself. When instead, he'd wanted Gia. The fire and the flame. What he'd always wanted.

Her survey of the crowd came to a halt when it reached him, her gaze meshing with his. The vulnerability on her face, the layer of confidence that had slipped, kicked him hard in the ribs. He had put it there—that uncertainty in her eyes. It sent a rush of anger pulsing through his chest.

His feet were moving before he'd fully registered it, carrying him through the packed, vibrating space. He reached the bottom of the stairs as Gia took her last step, his hands spanning her waist as he lifted her down. Hungry to see her, to touch her, to make things right between them, he kept his hands on her waist and pulled her close.

"You came," he murmured. "You look incredible."

"It's your big night. I didn't want to miss it." She tucked a chunk of her hair behind her ear in a nervous movement. "I'm sorry I'm late. My flight was delayed, then I had to get Leo to Chloe's. Then I couldn't find a dress that was right and I was going through Chiara's closet and I—"

He saw it then, the tears glittering in her eyes. The emotion bubbling beneath the surface. His heart beat a jagged rhythm in his chest as he pressed his fingers to the trembling line of her mouth, cutting her off midstream. "It doesn't matter. You're here. How is your mother?"

"Almost herself. She goes home tomorrow." She flicked a distracted look around them. "Is there somewhere we can talk?"

He wrapped his fingers around hers and led her through the thick throngs of partygoers to the small private lounge at the back of the club they'd used for media interviews. Directed her through the door and locked it behind them.

Filled with a tiny bar, a couple of sofas and a coffee table, and lit with low-light lamps, it was a small, intimate space. The silence between them as they turned to face one another was deafening. Unsure of what to do with his hands, because they wanted to be on her but they clearly needed to talk, he jammed them in his pockets.

"Gia—"

She held up a hand. "No. I have things to say. I need to get them out."

He didn't like the wounded, painful look in her eyes. Wanted to extinguish it. But since he was also responsible for it, he closed his mouth and forced himself to listen.

"I'm sorry I threw all of that at you on the

phone. I run, avoid my feelings, all of those things you say I do. But I was hurt. *Confused.*" She leaned back against the bar and raked a hand through her hair. "When you pushed me away after the dinner with Gervasio, I thought I'd broken something between us. It felt as if my marriage to Franco was happening all over again and I didn't know what to do about it. How to fix it. So I cooked you dinner that night. Which you blew off," she said, stating the painfully obvious detail he'd been kicking himself from here to Sunday for. "Then, when I called you in Munich, I heard Abigail in the background. Offering to introduce you to someone. As if the two of you were together."

He uttered an inward curse. He'd been so preoccupied with the party going on around him, about how lost she'd sounded, he hadn't even thought about it. For him, it had just been Abigail acting like the professional networker she was. "It was nothing," he said quietly. "You know that. You know *me*, Gia."

She shook her head. "I wasn't being rational. I was hurt. You had triggered all my insecurities the way you'd shut off on me." She dropped her gaze to the sparkling diamond on her hand.

Twisted it to sit straight. "After I failed to conceive a child for Franco, he withdrew. He called me frigid, *ice-cold*. The affairs," she conceded, "were a relief, because he left me alone. But they also decimated my self-confidence. I started to believe the things he was saying. How worthless I was. It didn't help," she added on an achingly vulnerable admission, "that I didn't have a very strong base to start with."

He hated himself so much in that moment, it was palpable. "I was trying to keep things afloat," he murmured. "Every time I engaged with you, we ended up in some deeply emotional place where I couldn't think. Couldn't function. Which wasn't a place I could allow myself to be. Not with everything riding on this launch."

She fixed steady green eyes on him. "I needed you."

That gutted him like a knife. He closed his eyes. Absorbed the far too powerful insight of hindsight. "It was my own history talking. *My* baggage talking, because it reminded me of my father. Of the relationship he and my mother shared." He blew out a breath, struggled for the words to explain. "It was passionate. Fiery. Never calm waters. Which only got worse when my father started his own company. My mother didn't want him to do it. She wanted him to stay on Wall Street, where the money was assured. But my father was addicted to the chase. To the *win*. He wanted this one to be his own.

"Their fights," he recalled, "were house-shaking affairs. Instead of having his eye on the business where it should have been, my father spent all of his time trying to keep my mother happy. The pressure—it was too much. He lost a big contract, one he'd bet the bank on, the business failed and he imploded."

Hurt flared in her dark eyes. "So you were afraid the same would happen to us? That I would be that destructive force for you?"

"All I could see," he said quietly, "in that moment, was that I was going to mess this up if I didn't rein it in. *Us*. This passionate relationship we share. So I shut myself down. Withdrew. It was wrong," he admitted. "If I could take it back, if I could do it all over again, I would, because I would never want to hurt you. *Ever*, Gia."

An emotion he couldn't read darkened her gaze. "What?" he prompted.

She drew in a deep breath. Issued a shaky exhale. "I'm afraid you're never going to let yourself feel the same way about me again," she said in an unsteady voice. "That I broke something between us when I walked away with Leo and I'm not sure you will ever let yourself go there again. That you will make this marriage work because you have to, but I will never be your *ideal* choice. I will be your *necessity.*"

He blinked as she threw that loaded statement at him. At how utterly and completely misguided it was. How it was equally his fault, because he'd let her go there.

She lifted her chin. "You had a list of the perfect woman, Santo. You rhymed it off to me countless times. She needs to be smart, with an impeccable social pedigree. Able to hold an interesting conversation over the dinner table with your business associates, but not too focused on business, because family takes priority. 'Martha Stewart by day, a sexual fantasy by night,' wasn't that how you put it? And then there was stipulation number four. She can't have too much *baggage*, because baggage is a *problem.*"

He absorbed his own words. It *was* his list. He knew it backward and forward. But none of it had ever mattered with Gia, because how he felt about her had always superseded rationality. He opened his mouth to tell her that, but she gave him a look that said let her finish.

"I am afraid," she said quietly, "that I will always be that political liability for you. That weak link, just like your mother was for your father. That every time we get somewhere good, *who I am* will destroy us. That it will break us over and over again until you decide you don't want me anymore."

He absorbed the heart-wrenching vulnerability on her face. How stripped down and bare she looked. It made his heart ache from deep within. And now, he decided, he'd had enough.

He stalked the few paces across the room and came to a halt in front of her. Stuck a hand on the bar beside her. "First of all," he said, "nothing your father ever says or does is going to break us. *Ever.* I promise you that. I signed Gervasio in Madrid, Gia. He's here tonight. He asked about you. So that is done. And when things get complicated in the future, which they will," he conceded, "because life is complicated, we will deal with it together.

"Secondly," he murmured, pressing a palm to her chest, absorbing the wild beat of her heart, "*this* is the only thing I care about. What's in here. Who you are. It's all I've ever cared about. And yes, I had a list. But you have always meant more to me than any list. You *supersede* it. It's why we keep coming back to each other time and again. Because no one else will do."

Her eyes widened into shining emerald orbs, glittering in the lamplight. "And finally," he said huskily, "I fell for you the first time I ever saw you, sitting at that cafeteria table by yourself. So brave. *Strong.* Determined not to let the world defeat you. And then," he added, "I watched you grow into this amazing woman, more comfortable in your skin with every day that passed. I told myself I couldn't have you. That you were promised to someone else. And then you kissed me in the elevator, and all my good intentions went out the window."

He brushed a thumb across her cheek, unable to resist touching her. "I was in love with you, Gia. I was going to go to your father the next morning and tell him you were marrying me, not Franco. But I never got the chance, because you walked away without a word."

Gia's heart tumbled right out of her chest and crashed to the shining dark oak floor. He'd been going to go to her father? *He'd loved her?* It was almost too much to imagine, how much she'd ripped apart, *destroyed*, by walking away.

"I didn't know," she whispered, lifting a hand to trace the sexy golden stubble on his jaw. "We didn't say anything that night."

A wry smile curved his mouth. "We were too busy doing other things…like making our beautiful son, who means everything to me."

A wave of heat engulfed her at the memory of that hot, torrid night. How perfect it had been. How it had changed her in every way. But it also unearthed the uncertainty of the past few weeks. All the nights he hadn't touched her since.

Santo read her in one even look. "You think I don't love you?" he said huskily, his hands cupping her cheeks. "You think I'm not crazy about you, Gia? You don't think I want you every minute I'm with you? When I saw you at that party in Nassau, I knew it wasn't over. That it would never be over for me. Why else," he prompted softly, "do you think I showed up at your doorstep at midnight like the raging bull that I was? Because it's always been you, Gia. It will always be you."

She sank into the wall, her knees weak. To

wonder about it for so long, to *dream* about it for so long, to be so afraid she was never going to hear him say those words to her, made it almost surreal to hear. Her heart was pounding so loudly in her chest, she thought it might thunder right out of it.

"I love you," she whispered. "So much it terrifies me. I always have."

He brought his mouth down on hers in a hot, hard kiss. She wound her arms around his neck and moved closer, her hands tangling in his hair as they exchanged soul-searing kisses, every hot breath, every stroke, every taste of each other a confirmation of what they were. What they could be. A consummation of the promises they'd made to each other.

"We should go back to the party," she murmured reluctantly against his mouth. "You are the host."

*"Later."*

Air became something she gasped in between indulging in the heated recklessness of his kiss. But soon even that wasn't enough. She wanted more—to obliterate the misery of the past few weeks. To drown herself in the connection they shared. To make *everything better.*

He took control, backing her up against the wall, his hands moving over her body in a sensual exploration that set her on fire. Caught up in the madness, desperate for him, she arched into his touch and sought closer contact. Begged him for more. The sparkly material of her dress a barrier to more intimate contact, he swept his hands up the back of her thighs and took the dress with him. Then it was only the hard, muscled length of him blanketing her with heat. He was hot and hard and she wanted him inside of her.

He palmed her thigh and curved it around his waist until she cradled the throbbing length of him at her core. Broke the kiss on a soft groan as she rocked against him in a rhythm that set him aflame.

"Santo," she whispered, eyes on his, "*love me.*"

"Always," he murmured, his gaze hot and smoky with passion.

And so he did, long and slow, every deep thrust, every achingly good caress, imprinting on her how much he loved her. Needed her. Cementing the bond they had always shared.

"I have to give a speech," Santo groaned when they finally came back from the sensual abyss, straightening their clothing with shaking hands. "A few more hours," he promised, "and I'm taking you and Leo home. And then *we* are spending a week at the villa in Nassau *alone*. And if I mention the word *Elevate* once, you can punish me. In all the right ways of course," he purred, sliding her a heated look as he straightened his tie.

Gia peeled her gaze away from how utterly gorgeous he looked in the dark grey suit, because he would always make her heart race like that. "A week alone?" The idea melted her insides.

"A belated honeymoon, courtesy of Delilah. No newspapers, no interruptions, just us."

She frowned as an obstacle to that plan presented itself. "What about my work with Nina? I've already been away a few days."

"I cleared it with her," her husband responded with his usual indomitable confidence. "I was prepared to spend the week convincing you to forgive me using whatever methods necessary."

She went a little weak at the thought of it. Which wasn't necessary, she conceded, because she loved and adored him. But this time, it was

288 MARRIED FOR HIS ONE-NIGHT HEIR

an adult love that had grown into everything she'd ever imagined it could be.

"Sold," she murmured, rising on tiptoe to give him a kiss. He returned it with a hard one of his own, then slipped his hand through hers as they walked toward the door.

"Ready?"

She nodded. She wasn't afraid of what was behind the door anymore, of what life would throw at her next, because she knew that whatever it was, she had Santo beside her and that was all that she needed.

Hand in hand, they walked into the buzzing, electric night. A tiny smile curved her lips as they joined her new family, congregated near the champagne fountain that threw up a luxurious, golden spray. Because this time, she was the girl at the center of the light.

\* \* \* \* \*